I0688495

DIAMOND STATE MAFIA

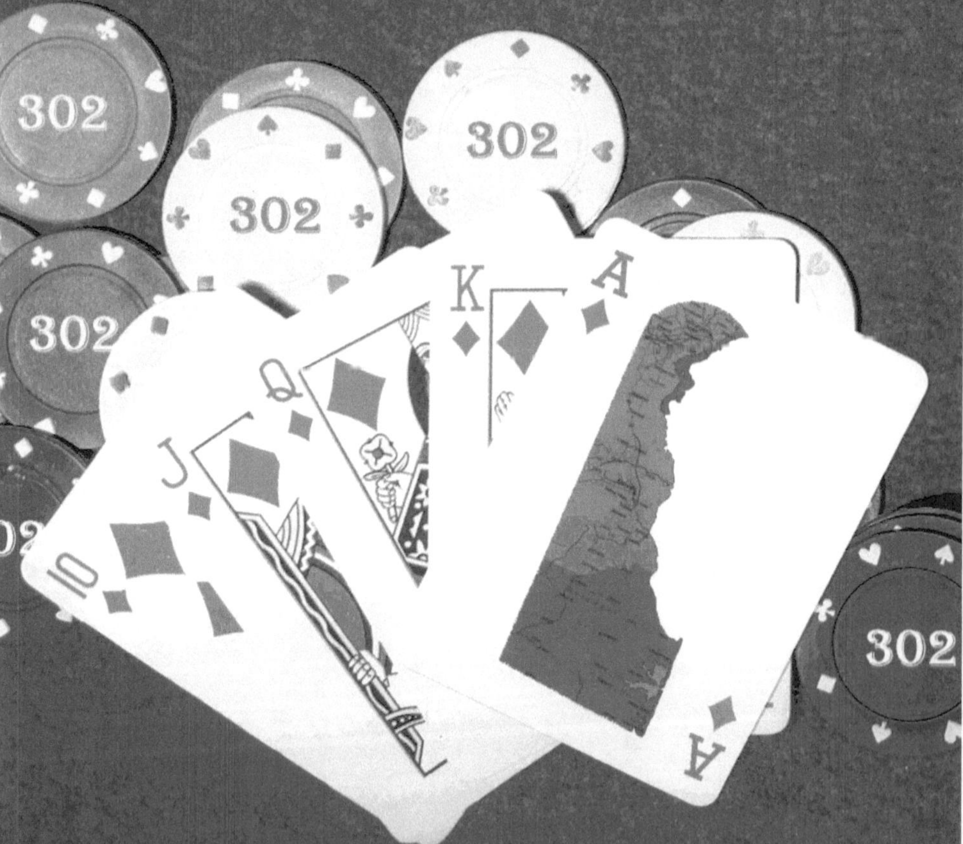

KYLEEF WATTS

Diamond State Mafia

By Kyleef Watts

Cover Created by Jazzy Kitty Publications

Cover Designed by Kyleef Watts

Logo Designs by Andre M. Saunders/Jess Zimmerman

Editor: Anelda L. Attaway

Co-Editor: Kyleef Watts

ACKNOWLEDGMENTS

First and foremost, I'd like to give thanks to the Creator for my gifts, blessings, trials, and tribulations!

I'd like to thank all the people that showed me love and encouraged me along this journey of LIFE. I couldn't have completed this book without my Coverdale Crossroads family.

Thank you, to the elders down to the kids!

Thanks for the support from all the people throughout the states of DE, MD & VA. From Seaford, Dodge City, Laurel, G. Town, Rehoboth, Dover, Wilmington, Milton, Milford, Woodside, Lincoln, Middletown, Smyrna, Ellendale, Williamsville, Salisbury, Cambridge, Hurlock, Federalsburg, Star Hill, Concord, Pine Town, Frankford, Selbyville, Accomac, VA Beach, and Norfolk.

Last but not least, my publisher Anelda Attaway and her staff at Jazzy Kitty Publications.

TABLE OF CONTENTS

TABLE OF CONTENTS

"Hello, this is your 911 dispatcher, Glades. What can I..." The calming voice of the dispatcher mid-sentence was abruptly interrupted.

"There's a home invasion taking place at this very moment, on 5th street in Blades at 1226!" Agent Rodgers ended the anonymous call he had made, shaking his head. The call was to the local police department. His superior wanted Agent Moore to remain embedded deep undercover to gain more intelligence and evidence against the Diamond State Mob, a moniker the FEDS coined for the organization beginning in Delaware. His superior's directive was "by no means should the targets know the FEDS are investigating."

The two agents watched four houses down from a black suburban, as the uniformed boys surrounded and charged into the small house. The agents watched as the notorious crew was frog marched out, single file and thrown into separate squad cars. The local officers high-fived and yelled, "Yahoo!" at the guest list of the well-known "so-called gangsters" they had collared. Agent Rodgers was just relieved that his fellow Agent Moore was able to get out of there unharmed. This was the first time in the two-year investigation that he had actually laid eyes on the crew. He knew most of the crew would be out of jail the next day.

He thought, *"So this what is money, drugs, and violence looks like?"*

Neighbors started to appear in windows and doorways. Some even came outside onto the red and blue-canvased lawns in the night. Agent Russell pulled off. The agents rode in the opposite direction content with their odds, which was a 98% conviction rate. Agent Rodgers loved the uncertainty and challenge, along with the adrenaline rush of being a Federal Agent. Rodgers thought of how great it's going to look on his resume when he cracks open the Diamond State Mafia case.

"This bust should be just enough to push me up the ladder to success." He couldn't wait to debrief Agent Moore.

Agent Russell asked, "Headquarters Boss?"

"No," Rodgers said, "we're gonna go to the jail and wait on all of them to get through receiving then debrief Moore."

8 Months Later

"WATSON! BAG YOUR BAGGAGE!"

Yusef Watson AKA X opened the electronic steel door to his cell with a smile. With a blanket as a knapsack thrown over his shoulder holding all his possessions, the once baldheaded bearded boss made his way through the desolate corridors to Booking and Receiving for his release. Along with the euphoric feeling of freedom at last, X also felt infuriated under his bright eyes. He took off the state's dingy white D.O.C. issued pants, V-neck t-shirt, socks, and boxers to change into his all-black L'Homme shirt and matching slacks with his black Clarks. His mind was on what The Family's lawyer told him the day before.

Michael Brewer ESQ, The Family's lawyer, stood in tan Roberto Cavalli monk strap shoes as X was led into the glass wall encased, small conference room. The correctional officer waited until X sat, then handcuffed the left wrist of the orange croc-wearing inmate to another set of cuffs, connected to a concrete wall. After the C.O. left the room, the lawyer shut the door. When he sat down face to face across from X a broad smile formed on his lips.

"I have good news and some bad news. Which one do you want first?"

X didn't hesitate, "The good news, my dude."

Michael's smile grew wider. "All the charges were officially dropped today. The DA fought as long and as hard as he could to pin Lil D's murder on you. But with all the dirty shit uncovered on Detectives Andies and Way, there was no way in hell anyone could cosign anything they touched. You'll be out of here tomorrow!"

The old friends were all teeth as they shook hands, causing the chains connected to X to rattle. Just as easy as Michael's smile was there, it disappeared.

"X...the night the state and local cops raided the house you were in...in Blades...in that room with you...one of them is an undercover federal agent..."

CHAPTER 1

Free

X stepped out of the prison doors holding nothing but a manila envelope containing his legal work. He stood still took a deep breath and closed his eyes pointing his face toward the sky. The early morning spring sun burned through a light fog. It had all the signs of a beautiful day to come. In the middle of him thanking his ancestors for giving him strength, a horn blowing made him look out into the parking lot. There sitting in a metallic, money green Beamer was his once best friend Kush. X just looked at Kush not moving a muscle. Kush blew the horn again as both men stared each other down. Kush had left X to die in the hands of the murderous Dominican twins Money and Fame. Afterwards, X was about to take Kush's life with Lana and the Family, just before the cops raided and began arresting everyone.

"C'mon Bro!" Kush yelled with a smile.

X slowly walked to the Beamer, opened the door to the *740Li* and plopped down into the seat. He just looked at the extended hand of Kush for a few moments before clasping his once closest friend hand. Both men faces broke into Kool-Aid smiles as Kush squealed wheels burning rubber exiting the prison grounds. They pulled out into the highway 1-13's traffic, marines with Big Money Grip's *"Red Rum"* pumping from the speakers.

"You thought it was me, didn't you?" X asked, "you thought I was a fucking FED!"

Kush looked puzzled then gave X a smile while shaking his head up and down before he spoke.

"Oh, so you know now?"

Kush turned the music down before he continued.

"Naw, I know it wasn't you Bro. But it could be Lana and I knew you wasn't letting nothing happen to your cuz."

X got hype and spoke aggressively with the mention of Lana. "Lana ain't no fucking Fed nigga! What the fuck is wrong with you?" Kush matched X's intensity and starkness.

"Well, shit was all good until the Queen B came along!" Kush paused only to light a blunt with his right hand as he held the stirring wheel with his left, "well, we got to get to the bottom of this shit..." He exhaled a cloud of smoke then continued, "plus, we gotta get our money back, and The Family ba..." X sat up straight in the seat cutting Kush off.

"Man, fuck The Family and that Money! Yes, we do have to get to the bottom of this undercover agent shit, but it ain't Lana!" He took the blunt as Kush passed it. "How did you know we were being infiltrated?" X asked. One pull from the blunt sent him into a coughing fit.

Kush laughed saying, "Boy, you got dem fresh lungs. That's that gas you smoking!" Kush answered X's question.

"El OSO has a FED in his pocket," in between coughing X manage to get out, "where's Evita and my son?"

The light-hearted laughter from X's choking episode only lasted a couple of seconds. Both men faces hardened. Kush looked at his childhood friend and seen the pain in X's eyes.

"I don't know, Bro..." X attempted to question Kush's honesty but Kush talked over him.

"Bro, you gotta know I would tell you if I knew!" Seeing X had calmed down, Kush continued, "I think El OSO exiled her back to the Dominican Republic."

X shot up so fast he jerked when the seatbelt caught him. "Take me to the Seaford Marina!"

Kush bust out in a hysterical laugh. "What the fuck you gonna do, sail there?"

"Hell Yeah!" X said sharply.

"Just give me a few days," Kush said pausing when he took a pull from the blunt, "I'm sure me and you…together can find out where they at."

X wasn't trying to wait for anything. He wanted Evita and his baby that he had never laid eyes on and he wanted to be away from any threats on his life. He yearned for peace, laughter, love and a future!

"MZ Rae and Kalana…that's all we gotta do…find them."

Kush was now pleading, "Bro, none of us want to be in this shit! I'm tired too. All of us was supposed to retire off that money, broski! Look...Let's finish what we started. We got in this with the goal of getting rich so we didn't have to do illegal shit. We right there, dog. A mile away from Heavens."

X frowned as he stared out of his passenger window. He hit the button to lower it. After seeing nothing but dullness for eight months, the colors from the Sussex County countryside popped out at him. The green and yellow cornfields were a magnificent blur, as they sped through the country. The fluffy white clouds in the marina blue sky felt like Déjà vu to X. Even the smell of the manure was welcomed by him and today smelled a little bit sweeter. He stuck his arm out of the window to feel the wind, the Freedom.

X's eight-month stint only gave him more time to think and come to the same conclusion of what he already knew, that his cheating death and avoiding life in prison days were numbered.

He thought to himself, *"I have a cool mil on the Clara Lee. I don't want money, even though two million sounds better than one."* X sat quietly nodding his head as he calculated how he could tie up all the loose ends.

"Alright, I will give Lana my word that her and MZ Rae are Family and are not a threat…and we gonna get this bread, TOGETHER!"

Kush smiled, "That's what I'm saying, my nigga. Family Love!" Kush's smile faded as X kept saying objectives.

"And that everyone in the Family will get a piece. A million apiece to the remaining founders and half a mil a piece to the soldiers."

Kush shook his head reluctantly in agreement passing the blunt back to X. They drove in silence each man puzzling together the pieces to their futures.

"We have to find out who this fuckin' Federal Agent is, 'cause we won't be sailing off in the sunset to enjoy that money if whoever it is isn't handled. We'll be rotting in a cell, 23 and 1!" Kush pulled up to a liquor store then turned to X.

"So you down Bro?" X clapped his hands and rubbed them together.

"Yes, but you gotta give me El OSO's head on platter! He's not gonna let me or Lana live in peace. Plus that fat puta tried to execute me."

Kush and X shook hands on it to seal the deal.

"What you want to drink Bro?" Kush asked getting out of the car.

X answered, "Get me a bottle of Pineapple Deep Flavor and some Belaire."

"OK," Kush replied turning to go into the store. Then he abruptly stopped and turned back around to X, "oh yeah Bro, you have a daughter not a son."

Lana stepped into her Netoure's Creation dress and shimmied it up over her round butt and curvy hips. She flattened out the wrinkles in her dress with her palms, as she stood in front of a hotel's vanity mirror. She then stepped into her Kate Spade black pumps and applied her red lipstick. While puckering up her lips in the mirror, her eyes looked past her own reflection to the dead body in the background.

The man was propped up against the headboard of the queen-sized bed. Lana turned to face the recently deceased former crack dealer. There was a perfectly centered bullet hole in his forehead. She took out her phone to call her cousin X.

"It's done," was all she said.

Lana hummed a carefree tune as she walked over to the side of the bed, only stopping to pick up a bulky titanium briefcase. She then walked out of the hotel room. X was sitting in a black Honda in front of the hotel's entrance. Lana smiled like a schoolgirl at seeing her cousin, especially after a job. She jumped in and handed him the heavy briefcase. He put the briefcase in the back seat. X clapped his hands then rubbed his palms together.

"I got something else for you, Cuz," X said with a sly grin.

Lana watched X as he reached down between his legs. Within the blink of an eye, Lana was staring down the barrel of a pistol. Before her eyes could relay what they were seeing to the brain, Lana saw the fire from the gun...BOOM! BOOM!

Lana's own screams jarred her from her nightmare. She sat up on a small thin plastic mattress on the floor. Her eyes searching every inch of the eight by ten room she was in. Lana tried with all her might to think and remember as she walked barefoot over a padded floor. It didn't dawn on her where she was until she reached the door of the small room. Lana put her face against the small window the door held then looked down at what she had on. Tears burst out of Lana's eyes as she wrung the gown she wore. She yelled and cried out until her lungs burned.

CHAPTER 2

Golden Eagle

"Damn, I wish X was here!" O.G. said out loud but to himself.

Icy Bezel nodded his head in agreement, knowing that what they were about to do was X's cup of tea. Icy Bezel and O.G. were laying down in a cornfield on the edge of a sprawling yard that held a turn of the century, renovated farmhouse deep in Camden Delaware's countryside. While X was in jail and Kush nowhere to be found, Icy Bezel, O.G., Isis, Kish, and Sista Vic set off to rebuild the once most prominent and ruthless organization in the state of Delaware.

"That was it, Bezel? Did you see it?" O.G. asked anxiously but at a whisper.

"Yeah, that was it."

The two had just seen a light in an upstairs room blink off and on three times. That was the signal they were waiting on from Isis and Kish. O.G. and Bezel back crawled a few feet before they stood up and walked through the cornfield to the other side, where they had a Crown Vic parked. There they stood at the car's opened trunk, suiting up. They retrieved handcuffs, zip ties, Tasers and 45 caliber pistols from the trunk. Each of them wore vests that read ICE on the front along with black fatigues and gold badges dangled from the necklaces around their necks. They got into the car and drove a quarter mile around the cornfields and woods to the farmhouse they were watching minutes prior. O.G. cut the red and blue emergency lights on as he gunned the engine of the Crown Vic, turning off the road onto a long dirt lane. The cop car roared as it approached the house. The car was yanked into park, a split second before the men were out and up to the front door.

Icy Bezel and O.G. yelled in unison, "IMMIGRATION!" as O.G. kicked the door two times before it flew off its hinges.

Tykisha Moore AKA Kish's happiest and darkest memories of her life flashed before her eyes as she squeezed the trigger of the tiny, small two-shot Dillinger. Only inches from the back of a naked Cholo's head, Kish had to make a spilt second decision. Either let O.G. and Icy Bezel get killed or break an oath by committing murder. Without hesitating or questioning her involuntary movements, Kish closed her eyes and squeezed the trigger twice. The headshots instantly killed the Mexican. As the dead Cholo fell forward down the remaining steps to the first floor of the farmhouse, Kish's thoughts were already on the ramification and consequences of the act she'd just committed.

A naked Isis and Kish rushed down the stairs, just as Icy Bezel grabbed the assault rifle that the dead Cholo dropped as he tumbled down. Just a second ago, the Mexican was spraying the AR-15 down the stairs, shredding the furniture and walls of the living room in an attempt to kill the intruders Icy Bezel and O.G. Blood saturated the beige carpet as it expanded outward, touching Kish's bare feet. Her 5'4 chocolate body glistened from sweat, as she looked down not able to look away from the dead Mexican. Tears welled up in her eyes as Kish's mind rewound back four years earlier to her graduation.

The 20 people all rose to their feet from the aluminum fold-up chairs to applaud the newly sworn-in Federal Agents. George Rodgers beamed like a proud father as Tykisha Moore made eye contact with him from the small stage. After the service Kish weaved through the small crowd of her fellow agents and their supporters until they met with an embrace.

"I know your grandfather's looking down on you smiling," said George Rodgers as he walked arm-in-arm with Tykisha. It was George, or rather Uncle G, as Tykisha called him that persuaded her to apply to be a Federal Agent.

"Your Grandfather looked out for me and took me under me his wing, when I was a snot-nosed beat cop rookie," George stopped her by gently grabbing Kish's arm; when he had her attention and eye contact he continued, "you'll be in the Thief and Merchandise Division."

Tykisha beamed with confidence so proud of her accomplishment. It melted the veteran agent Rodgers' heart. She was ecstatic about her new job. Rogers was all she had since her grandmother passed a year ago and she was all he had since being divorced. George had pulled some strings to get her in that department because it was very low risk to violence. He wouldn't dare put her in a dangerous situation.

Kish's jubilation and enthusiasm didn't last long for her new job. Within months she was bored out of her mind with the tedious white-collar fieldwork. Kish longed for some action. Her prayers were answered after meeting a young high school graduate, by the name of Kalana Watson. While working undercover as a department store manager on the lookout for fraud, Kish befriended her. Kish remembered the adrenaline rush she had when her Uncle G finally gave in and took her suspicions and observations serious. Kish had already been reporting to her Uncle, off the record, on how Kalana went from a timid, penniless sweetheart to having a house, new cars and the confidence of a lioness. Kish thought back and came to the conclusion that Kalana's fortunes and attitude changed, after they had met her long-estranged cousin Yusef. With the mention of Yusef Watson's name, Kish saw her Uncle G give her his undivided attention. The following day Tykisha Moore was officially transferred to the DEA in her uncle Agent Rodger's unit.

Kish snapped out of her daze to hear Icy Bezel and Isis arguing.

"Damn, that crazy ass Mexican almost shot us! What the fuck y'all was doing?" Icy Bezel said vehemently, not loud but aggressively while pulling off his mask.

"Shut up Bezy!" Isis shot back, "my bitch just saved yo ass!"

Kish noticed O.G.'s attention was on her and Isis's naked bodies.

"So where the shit at?" O.G. asked his eyes never going above the girls' shoulders. Isis and Kish lead O.G. and Icy Bezel upstairs to the bedroom where they were entertaining the now dead Cholo.

The bedroom, just like the house was basic and modest having the minimum of luxury furniture and comfort. A queen-sized bed and a dresser, covered in white and yellow candles, were the only pieces of furniture in the room. Kish picked up her clothes that were scattered around the room as Isis led Icy Bezel and O.G. to a closet. There wasn't a door on the closet. A rainbow of colorful beads was its only barrier. The sound of the beads as Isis parted and stepped through them, was the only sound breaking the eerie silence. Inside was a table with a white sheet covering it that hung to the floor. Mounds of lit and melted candles of all colors painted the table cover. There were also various foods, fruits and a half-smoked cigar.

"Poppi always did this when he came in here." Isis made the sign of the cross over her body while saying a prayer.

"No disrespect to the Orishas!"

Icy Bezel and O.G. stood behind Isis single file in the walk-in closet and exchanged looks. They watched as the petite stark, naked Isis bent down and slowly moved the white sheet up from the floor. Isis' small, delicate hand disappeared from O.G. and Icy Bezel's vision for a few seconds. She grunted while struggling, before a chest was revealed from beneath the Alter. The lit candles flickered as the chest slid over the floor.

Kish got fully dressed in a dark but colorful Holt Renfrew dress. Her red Prada heels dangled from her fingers as she sat on the edge of the bed. Her mind, along with her emotions, was in overdrive. In the mist of the sea of feelings and images, faces of her grandparents, Lana and the Mafia appeared. She envisioned her Uncle G's eyes that held disappointment and made her feel like her heart had been stabbed. Kish had come to look at Isis as a sister and the Mafia as her family. Kish's eyes popped wide open when the reality of her situation fought through all the gray area and fence straddling, to reveal a clear and unfiltered profile of a common sociopath.

"We back!" Isis screamed as she came through the beads first, followed by a hunched over O.G. carrying a handle on one end of the 4x4 chest with Icy Bezel heaving on the other end.

"I hope this heavy mafucka' filled with cash!" Icy Bezel said to O.G.

Isis, still naked, danced in front of Kish sitting on the bed.

"Put some clothes on, girl! You crazy!" Kish said pushing her friend playfully as she jumped off the bed, trying to match Isis' excitement at seeing the boys drop the heavy chest to the floor. Isis got dressed quickly while the rest of the Fam examined the locked chest.

"Stand back!" O.G. said as he fired two shots into the lock mechanism.

"That shit always work in the movies!" he said when he saw that nothing changed.

The leather covered iron chest didn't show any signs of the shots from the pistol.

"Kish," Isis said as she shimmied up her skirt, "get the key from around poppi's neck. You know where he always keep it."

Isis hurriedly pulled on her silk Etro blouse, with an innocent looking but devilish smile on her face reminiscent to a mischievous schoolgirl. Since the Family had fallen apart, Isis and the others were living in poverty. The thousands and thousands of dollars that was once spent effortlessly and without caution was just a memory now. Isis was anxious to get back to living like a goddess and being able to possess anything she desired.

Kish felt as if she was having what they call an out-of-body experience. She watched all the events of herself and the Family from above. She heard Isis giggle as she continued to see from a bird's eye view, as her own body floated down the stairs. Kish felt numb, no pain physically or emotional nor any thoughts on whether things were good or bad. To her, her limbs were moving involuntary. Kish watched herself snatch the beaded necklace off of the Mexican's neck that held a six-inch skeleton key. In what felt like a blink of an eye she was back upstairs handing the key to Icy Bezel. While everyone else crowded around the chest, Kish examined the blood on her hands, slowly turning them over.

"What have I done?"

The key turning into the lock and the creak of the hinges sounded amplified in the quit room as Icy Bezel opened the chest. Icy Bezel, O.G., and Isis simultaneously shouted out in joy at seeing the chest filled to the brim with white squares. Their jubilation was short lived.

"Wait! Wait! Wait!" O.G. said as he picked up two of the kilos, one in each hand, "Look!" He pointed to the symbol in the center of one of the bricks out to Icy Bezel.

Icy Bezel took another brick from the chest and held it closer to his face, studying what looked like a big bird. "These bitches den got us in some shit!" Icy Bezel said flatly shaking his head looking at Isis and Kish.

O.G. started throwing a barrage of questions to both women.

"How y'all know this dude? Did somebody put y'all on to him? How'd y'all know about all this?"

Neither woman answered his questions. Isis spoke up. "We got like…50 keys Boy, chill out."

Trying to smile off the straight faces on O.G. and Icy Bezel. In the blink of an eye Icy Bezel had his hands around Isis' small neck. O.G. tried to intervene but Icy was furious and locked on. Just as fast as it had started, Icy Bezel stopped but was still as a mannequin. It was only when Icy removed his hands from Isis' neck that the others could see the straight razor held to his own. Isis' razor was firm up against the side of Icy Bezel's neck.

When she removed it panting, a line of blood formed on his neck. "Nigga, don't you eva fuckin' touch me!"

O.G., talking to both of them said, "You two Muthafuckas crazy! Let's get this and bounce.

"We ain't good, dog!" Icy Bezel said as he pointed to the symbol. "Do you know what this is?"

Isis replied with a smirk, "Yeah, a bird."

Kish stayed quite, but she knew what the symbol represented.

Throwing the kilo back in the chest, Icy Bezel spat. "That's a fucking Golden Eagle!"

Isis' facial expression was like "so what".

O.G. explained as he closed the chest and started dragging it out the room, "That's the emblem of The Mexican Mafia, LA EME!"

CHAPTER 3

Delaware City

Attorney Jerry Weston's strides were long, hard and purposeful in his black, double-breasted custom-tailored Sean John suit. He burst through the double doors of Delaware City's top psychiatric institution with papers in hand. An equally conservative, yet impressively dressed tall, slender black female followed behind the lawyer. Jerry Weston didn't wait for a response from the nurse at the desk.

"This is a court order from the Honorable Oscar T. Getter! It states that one Kalana R. Watson is to be release immediately from your care!"

Weston and his companion then stormed right past the nurse as she called after them. "Mister. MISTER! Ma'am... You can't go down there!"

After entering the wing that read CHRONIC CARE, Weston presented the court order to another nurse that sat behind a desk. The young lady in the blue scrubs seemed eager to help.

"Follow me," the full-figured young nurse said curling her index finger.

She led them down a long hall that held rooms on either side. The lawyer and his lady companion heard screams coming from some of the rooms and in others they saw faces pressed against the glass of the small 10-inch windows.

"She's in here," the nurse said as she reached for the doorknob, "I'm so glad somebody came for her." The nurse opened the door and stood back, letting them go first as if she was expecting something.

"Who are YOU?" Weston spat entering the room.

In there, Lana was in restraints and a large White man was sitting in a chair beside her.

The man shot to his feet when Weston and the lady barged into the room. "I'm Special Agent George Rodgers!" the athletic built man who looked to be in his late 40s said as he whipped out his credentials.

The Attorney Weston stepped forward coming face to face with the Agent.

"This is against the LAW!"

A swarthy Lana was confined to a desk-like chair that restrained its occupant's hands, feet and head. Lana's head was reclined back awkwardly. A hint of a smile flickered on her lips. Lana struggled to open her heavy red eyes.

"Oh my GOD!" The lady with the Attorney said at seeing Lana.

"There's no harm in a social visit," Agent Rodgers said continuing to make eye contact with Weston as he walked out the small room.

"Rae… is that you for real?" Lana asked hoarsely.

"Yes Baby, we taking you home," said MZ Rae sobbing while her fingers moved fast to free Lana's wrist and ankles.

"How do I know you are real this time and not my mind playing tricks on me?" Lana asked with a sly smile just as MZ Rae unloosened her.

"Because of this!" MZ Rae hugged and squeezed Lana as tight as she could, "come on, Girl! Let's go shopping, get your nails done and hair did…." MZ Rae helped her to her feet.

Weston gave MZ Rae his suit jacket and she put it over Lana's shoulders and held her friend close as they walked out of the mental hospital. Before Weston could pull the Audi truck carrying MZ Rae and Lana out of the parking lot, the blond-haired young nurse came running towards them.

"Hey, MZ…MZ….!" The nurse stopped at the back window and held a plastic bag up. After MZ Rae's window went down the nurse handed her the bag. "They've been withholding her meds from her for two days. She has to take one of these every day in order for her to be normal."

The nurse's eyes welled up with tears as she nervously smiled and waved, "Goodbye Kalana…!"

"Where the hell have you been? You've missed the last two fuckin' check-ins!" Agent George Rodgers hissed at Kish through clenched teeth. The two agents were at a cozy restaurant in Ellendale Delaware called the Southern Grill. Kish sat across from Agent Rodgers concealing her identity as much as she could by wearing sunglasses and an oversized hoodie.

Kish responded back defensively. "I'm the one out there with my life on the line!"

Agent Rodgers had watched Kish through the restaurants window when she had arrived. He was well aware of the change in her body language and now listening to her talk it was apparent that she wasn't the same person.

"Maybe I should pull you…" Rodgers said before Kish cut him off.

"Uncle G I can do this," Kish said now, removing her shades, "the Family is about to do something BIG!"

Agents Rodgers stirred his coffee while looking into Kish's eyes. "Right now YOU have nothing!" He took a sip from his cup and then continued, "Let me have the video you recorded of the Mafia purchasing from our Mexican informant."

For a moment Kish was at a loss of words. "I…I…I don't have it."

Agent Rodgers voice carried over the rest of the patrons in the restaurant. "WHAT?!"

Kish lied, "They made men sit that one out."

Agent Rodgers rubbed his head and massaged his temples in frustration.

Kish kept talking fast. "Uncle G, they're having a Family meeting coming up real soon. Everyone is gonna be there. I haven't seen X since his release or Lana yet but Isis said the whole Family will be there." Kish saw that Rodgers was listening. "They HAVE to get the money…so if not anything, we can get all of them on tax evasion and the RICO. I'll record the meeting."

Agent Rodgers sat quietly for a moment. Kish couldn't read his aquiline face. "Kish, if nothing develops from this…Imma PULL you MYSELF!" The veteran agent said as he stood up. "I haven't heard anything from our Mexican informant…if them phony black mafia punks tried that robbery shit with those crazy son of a bitches they'll be sorry. Those spics don't play!"

Kish looked down into her own cup of coffee. "I don't know Sir, it's a possibility." Kish couldn't dare look up to meet Rodgers eyes as he stood in front of her. She could feel his eyes boring down into her head.

"Huh," was all that Agent Rodgers said before he stepped off.

Tucked into the secluded back roads, deep in the woods of Accomac, Va., was where MZ Rae lived. What felt like the first time in years, Lana woke up comfortably in a queen-sized bed. She felt refreshed. Lana rubbed her thighs feeling her soft skin. She inhaled deeply, smelling a sweet gentle fragrance.

"I smell like a real woman!" Lana stretched, yawned, and her eyes popped wide-opened as if she was expecting to snap out of this serene dream to see her bleak and dull reality. Instead, she opened her eyes to see a room that could have been decorated by Martha Stewart. The picturesque, neat room was peppered with pictures and African American knickknacks all over the cherry wood dressers and stands. A gap in the burgundy curtains in the window beside her bed showing the spring countryside convinced her that this wasn't a dream.

"I couldn't even imagine a place that screams HOME so much," Lana said.

A big smile spread across Lana's face when she realized that she had been asking herself the same question every morning when she woke up for the past week.

"Is this REAL?"

She smelled breakfast cooking and heard the radio on downstairs. Lana could faintly hear 101.7's Kola On-Air saying something about a coming home party for X this weekend in Groove City. Lana heard footsteps getting closer, like someone was running up the stairs.

MZ Rae bust through the half-opened door. "Did you hear that?" she asked Lana.

"I know I was hearing right," Lana said throwing the covers off of her and springing out of bed.

"You going?" MZ Rae asked looking worried knowing what the

answer was going to be.

"Yes!" Lana said shaking her head slowly as if convincing herself.

"We're going," Lana said more confidently.

MZ Rae shook her head as she turned, walking back down the hall and down the stairs to the kitchen. Lana followed her friend knowing what she was thinking. The last time MZ Rae had seen X and the other Family members they wanted Sizzle's combination of numbers so they could get the millions of dollars that were in an offshore account. It was evident that the Family would of killed MZ Rae after she gave up the numbers. Lana was the only reason MZ Rae was alive.

Lana continued, "Well, you said yourself that you need X and Kush's numbers to get the money."

MZ Rae's only response was to push her Gucci glasses up at the bridge of her nose, while she opened the refrigerator to get some orange juice. "Lana, excuse my French but fuck that!"

Lana bust out laughing, MZ Rae cussing always sounded funny. MZ Rae even smiled at her own expense herself but was dead serious. "For real Lana! We Living! I survived by the grace of GOD…and you…" MZ Rae paused for a second, as a picture from the night the Dominicans bum rushed the mansion and killed Sizzle ran through her mind. A cold chill made her body shudder before she could continue, "…for not letting me get killed."

Lana waved MZ Rae off. "Rae you saved me…from that insane asylum."

Both women shook their heads. "Oh, get me my pills girl…you know I'm crazy."

"You are not crazy girl," MZ Rae demanded. MZ Rae continued to talk as she walked into the living room, "Lana, I don't care about the money. Our lives are at stake!"

She stooped to one of the large vases that sat on each sides of her fireplace. She parted the natural branches then reached her hand down into the vase to retrieve a small pill bottle. MZ Rae opened it and took out one tiny white pill. She put the cap back on then placed the bottle back where it was in the vase. MZ Rae walked back into the kitchen to find Lana already eating the breakfast she had cooked. She gave Lana the pill and her friend took it immediately. MZ Rae sat down across from Lana to her own plate of grits, turkey bacon, beef sausages and fried potatoes.

"And Lana…you don't need any money with the investments I've made with your money."

Lana knew she didn't need the money. When she was first committed to the mental institution Lana appointed MZ Rae as her power of attorney over all of her properties and accounts. Lana told MZ Rae a couple weeks later where most of her money was buried on those properties. MZ Rae's knowledge and education of commerce, capitalism, and love of numbers, along with stocks and bonds, was able to be put to work. By having Lana's long money she was able to make lucrative investments in real estate and together they owned the majority of shares of two national restaurant chains. MZ Rae handled Lana's money with care like it was her own. By the time she was able to get Lana released, MZ Rae had quadrupled her friend's money.

Lana wasn't worried about The Family's money or the portion that her and MZ Rae could get from it. Lana missed the 24/7 adrenaline rush. She missed the guns, the fear and the blood. She craved for some action. The once innocent girl that was motivated by money was now fueled by hate. Hate for all greedy men with power and money that think they could just do anything to women. Lana snapped out her daze, where she relived getting raped and her finger cut off.

Lana interrupted MZ Rae who was talking all the while she was in one of her small blackouts, "Imma go to see X at his coming home party…It's my homecoming too! Plus, I'll get the rest of the numbers to the account and get that money!" Lana said moving her head side-to-side dramatically and poking her lips out when she said, "Money!"

MZ Rae just shook her head and couldn't help smiling at her silly friend.

"You are crazy," MZ Rae said as both women bust out laughing.

Lana couldn't help but think in the back of her mind that X having a party and have it being promoted on the radio was a call out for her anyway.

CHAPTER 4

Brooklyn Boy

"The Family is back!" like Isis had said and they were.

With the twenty kilos they took from that Mexican, they immediately went to work. The crew split Delaware in half. Isis and O.G. took the north end from Woodside to Wilmington. Kish and Icy Bezel had Milford to Delmar. The Family hit every nook and cranny in the state.

Just like DMX's chorus said, "Stop, drop, shut 'em down, open up shop!" The Family distributed their product from city blocks to country holes.

With the Family back in action and eating on the streets that meant somebody's pockets were coming up short. A hustler from Brooklyn by the name of Coco had filled the void of narcotics on the streets when the Family crumbled. He felt a tremendous decline in clientele and money. Coco had a team of vicious young Brooklynites that he had down from the city. They had never seen the amount of money that they were making down here in the "boondocks" as they say. His team was peppered throughout Kent and Sussex County. They all reported the same sad news to their big homie, that business had slacked up in the last three weeks.

Coco stayed with NeNe, a local girl from southern Delaware. NeNe knew X, Kush, Icy Bezel and all the other Family members. She was a regular home girl to the Family, from around the way. NeNe told Coco all about the Family and all its members. All what she heard and all she knew. NeNe also told him that X was having a coming home party in a couple of days. She had met Coco on his first OT trip to Delaware. New York hustlers had been coming to Delaware since the crack era erupted in the early eighties.

NeNe loved Coco's New York swagger and Brooklyn attitude. From the way he spoke to the style of clothes he wore. To her Coco was the epitome of a gangster. NeNe had been living in the projects with her two kids until she met Coco. She had been barely living above poverty, surviving off welfare and state assistance when Coco came along. Coco insisted that she keep the crib in the projects but put her and the kids in a townhouse. Coco had brought her a car and bills weren't an issue anymore. NeNe had never had so many new, fresh clothes and shoes. To her Coco was a savior and NeNe would do anything for him.

X's Coming Home party was held at the Hookah Lounge in Cambridge, Maryland. The Eastern Shore's elite came out to celebrate with him. People as far as north Philly and as far south as VA, came looking like new money. DJ X Lethal manned the ones and two's to the packed turnout. The building was near its capacity and many more partygoers stood outside in a seemingly endless line.

Promoter Rico Reef stood outside the clubs doors with two huge bouncers flanking him. "You right there in the fishnets. You and your girls come on."

One of the big men unhooked a velvet rope to let the five-woman entourage in. Fresh to death men and women in designer suits, denim, dresses and skirts, took selfies and talked as they waited for a chance to get in. The footwear ranged from boots, sneakers and heels. Some guys had a mean shoe game. Some were permitted to pass while others were turned away and some yelled out obscenities at Rico for being rejected. Lana walked pass hundreds of men and women in the line that led up to the clubs entrance. Dudes turned and had rubbernecks while some women gave envious looks as Lana confidently walked in a powder pink Ruched Dolce & Gabbana dress. The sheer dress gave glances of her cleavage and thighs as she walked with an heir of importance.

"Kalana, what's up your highness," Rico said with a big smile.

"Super Promoter Rico, what's up handsome," Lana said as the two embraced.

Rico whispered in her ear. "X said go back to your car and read this." Rico palmed a tiny piece of paper into Lana's hand on the sly.

When she got back into her all white G wagon, Lana unfolded the small piece of paper. "THE CAVE!" was the entire message read.

An hour later, Lana was in Delaware to an apartment complex they called Da Gardens. The Cave was one of numerous safe houses that the Family once owned.

"I didn't know X still had this," Lana said to herself as she did a drum roll like knock on the door.

Memories of Stretch made her inhale deep. She shook her head as she exhaled and her heart skipped a beat as she thought about Stretch's gentle touch. Before the door ever opened she heard Sista Vic's laughter. But once the door swung open Sista Vic had a straight face.

Lana just stood there like a deer in headlights. She didn't know what to expect from Sista Vic. The two looked at each other in silence for a couple seconds before a smile formed on Sista Vic's face and then she opened her arms wide to hug Lana.

"Come on in baby!" Lana heard a song by Betty Wright being played and an array of delicious aromas hit her nose as she stepped into the apartment.

She started to open her mouth to greet Sista Vic as she followed her into the kitchen but Lana's words were clipped short.

"How have you been..."

At Sista Vic's kitchen table, Isis and Kish sat with plates and bowls full of colorful foods in front of them. Before the silence had time to become awkward Sista Vic intervened.

"Come on Lana, pull up a chair." Lana sat at the small round table facing both Isis and Kish. The two didn't look up at Lana, their faces stayed on the food they were eating.

"Let me tell y'all little bitties something," Sista Vic said with one hand on her hip and the other holding a fork turning over fried chicken over her stove, "we have a lot of frog skins on the line. Y'all kiss and make up or do whatever y'all used to do because we can't get paid unless we're TOGETHER!"

She turned around from the stove to look at all three women. Sista Vic stood with her head cocked to the side and both hands on her hips. Waiting. Finally Kish extended her hand over the table towards Lana.

"It's good to see you, Lana," Kish said.

She smiled nervously when Lana reached over the table to shake her hand. Kish didn't care that Lana had given her, her left hand. She had actually missed Lana and felt terrible how she had treated her. No smile cracked Lana's beautiful face. Her Clinique foundation and make-up was flawless.

Isis stood up and circled the table until she was standing over Lana. Lana was taken off guard when Isis bent down and hugged her tight. "I'm so sorry, sister!" Tears flooded from Isis' eyes.

"It's alright, Ice," Lana said standing up embracing Isis, she patted and rubbed her once partner in crime's back.

As Isis returned to her seat, she noticed Lana's facial expression hadn't changed at all. Lana still had the same emotionless look on her face.

"Heeey!" Sista Vic yelled, happily clapping her hands. Still grinning, excited that her Family was back together. Sista Vic said, "Queen B, go over to Da Cave to get the boys. Everybody's already here. We were waiting for you. X knew you would come."

"Son, we been waitin' out here for a minute! You gon let the Gods in or WHAT?"

"It's packed to full capacity, bro. Fire marshals threatening to shut me down now."

Coco and three of his NYC goons stood outside the velvet ropes of the Hookah Lounge. Rico Reef's two bouncers stepped to the forefront when the New York natives didn't budge.

"Is that nigga X in there?" Coco asked.

From the man's tone and the disposition of his crew, Rico knew these weren't X's friends or fans.

"Naw My G, you just missed him."

Before the words came off Rico's lips Coco had brandished a huge nickel-plated revolver. Like a domino effect, each man with Coco pulled out his own pistol as well.

"I wanna check fo' myself B," Coco said as he cocked the hammer back on his gun.

"Brotha, do whateva you feel!" Rico said as he and the bouncers moved to the side.

X held a finger up telling everyone at the table and around the room to be quiet. He was in Da Cave surrounded by all the Family members, the founders, himself, Kush, and Icy Bezel. The matriarch, Sista Vic, O.G., Lana, Isis, and Kish the soldiers were all there. They all had made amends if for nothing at all, the money. Each Family member got a chance to voice his or her opinions and wishes.

While X and Kush were explaining to the others how the millions would be divided up, Rico Reef called.

"What up Rico Reef!"

"Yo Big Homie, some thugged out ass New York niggas up here looking for you!"

X's face creased as he frowned, knowing this was going to be some bullshit. Before he could ask who and why, shots were heard from the other end of the line.

"O SHIT!"

X and the others heard Rico say as he was placed on speaker, "These New York muthafuckas shootin…"

Rico didn't say anything else. From then on the Family just heard muffled sounds, faint screams and loud music before the call was ended. Isis and Kish's eyes briefly darted towards one another for a split second while O.G. and Icy Bezel both shook their heads.

"What?" X asked seeing everyone's silent response. Bezel just bit on the tip of the black and mild cigar in his mouth. "What dem niggas looking for me for?" X asked shaking his head with a smile of disbelief.

"Dem cats set up shop right after we fell off," O.G. said next.

"But we back now…"

Isis abruptly cut O.G. off moving her head from side to side like a snake, "And them sorry funny style ass muthafuckas ain't gettin' no more Money!"

Everyone in the room laughed at Isis' bluntness. The comedy in the mist of talking money and violence wasn't new to anyone in the room. It felt like old times to the once tight knit group. X couldn't lie to himself as he looked around the smoke-filled room. He definitely missed the comradeship and the "us against the world" feeling he had, knowing that all his loved ones were finally good and would have his back to the death.

Just as fast as the euphoric, natural high that a hustler feels counting money climaxed, it receded. A vision of Evita holding a fat caramel complexioned, wavy haired baby, slid over X's eyes and then was gone. The split-second image was as massive as a punch to the face. "Evita!" X's inner voice screamed out.

Before the Family dispersed for the night a final discussion was held about the Families millions in the Cayman's. X, Kush, and Icy Bezel wrote down their codes on the front of a Big Money Grip CD cover. Icy Bezel was the last to write down his numbers down. He slid the CD cover across the table to Lana aggressively. Lana narrowed and rolled her eyes at him. Icy Bezel gave her back a mean scowl. Lana was going to deliver the codes to MZ Rae. In one week they would meet up to split the money.

CHAPTER 5

Clarity

Kish pulled off of Route 13 in Seaford, Delaware. She drove through the small city ending up right off the Nanticoke River, at an old warehouse. Some of the buildings go back to the civil war. This was once a major port for the shipment of supplies to troops, and equally important afterwards for commerce and trade. It now looked ghost, like it hadn't been inhabited in over 50 years.

Kish used a key to open up a side door at one of the dull gray buildings. The inside was the complete opposite to its industrial blue-collar outer appearance. Custom office furniture adorned the inside. She walked down a long-carpeted hallway until it opened up to a small room that held about six chairs, all facing a 6x4 dry erase board. The board held pictures of all the remaining members of the Diamond State Mafia. Under each photo were notes written in red marker.

Kish hadn't been here in months, her eyes scanned over all the information the board held directly because of her. One picture got her attention, Kalana Watson. The paragraphs and underlines were longer and more than any other Family members.

Kish started to read what was under Lana's name. *"-MURDERS TWO DOMINICANS-MARKET ST WILMINGTON DE-PEPE SANCHAZ AND JESUS FERNANDES-MURDER TWO BLACK MALES-SALISBURY MD-ANDRE AG GENTRY AND ANTONIO DIGGS – MULTIPLE MURDERS-VIRGINIA BEACH VIRGINIA-GREGORY NICE CANNON AND ELLA MEA CANNON-"* Kish read out loud to herself, information she hadn't given her superiors nor did she even know about.

Agent George Rodgers interrupted Kish with the clearing of his throat behind her. "Ugh um ummm..." Kish spun around.

"Good morning Uncle G...Excuse me, Special Agent Rodgers," Kish said giving him a smile.

Agent Rodgers just grunted his hello and said sarcastically, "You must most definitely have something gigantic, to grace us with your presence, coming in here smiling...in My FBI headquarters?"

"You know I haven't had a chance to get away," Kish answered still with that innocent smile she knew melted her uncle G's defenses.

She had been giving that innocent smile since him and his ex-wife had been taking her to the state fair, once a year after her grandfather passed away. Kish turned her attention back to the board. She unclasped her Michael Kors watch and held it up as she continued to read Lana's history.

Agent Rodgers closed the small gap between the two of them with one long step. Their tech guy, Agent Russell, put video, audio surveillance and recording devices in a lot of accessories that Kish carried. Pens, earrings, sunglasses, phones, belt buckles and watches.

"Is this the vigilante guy meeting?" Agent Rodgers asked finally showing his coffee stained teeth with a grin that looked painful, "was it the whole gang?"

"Yes Sir," Kish replied.

"Russell should have been here," Rodgers said checking his watch as he walked to his office further into the warehouse.

"I need to hear their next move and can't do it without this egghead."

"Sir, Sir?" Kish called.

"What?" Rodgers answered as he was placing his suit coat on the coat stand in his office.

"You have some more info for me?"

"I Might!" Kish yelled back before she continued, "where did you get all this intel on Kalana Watson?"

Rodgers came back into the room with Kish. He emptied the old coffee grinds and was busy making a fresh pot. Rodgers whistled Bobby Mcferrin's "Don't Worry, Be Happy."

Kish turned to Rodgers. "Is this info real?" That question got a reaction from Rodgers.

"You bet your ass its real Sweetheart. I got it from the Queen Bitches own twisted ass lips!"

"Lana...I mean Kalana told you this?" Kish looked questionable at the linebacker shaped Agent. "How?"

Rodgers ignored her question and asked one of his own. "Sugar and cream?"

"Yes!" Kish said feeling agitated that she couldn't get a straight answer, "do you have something more than a bunch of talking? I'm talking bout a hand in the cookie jar red-handed bust!" Rodgers knew Kish was holding back on the intel of the Family.

"Actually it's something going down tonight."

Kish was quiet now after receiving a cup of coffee from her superior officer. He stayed quiet, waiting for Kish to reveal her information before he showed his hand.

"I can get you Icy Bezel with nothing less than a kilo, red handed."

Rodgers shook his head while savoring his first sip of coffee. He turned and walked back to the same table that held the coffee pot. Rodgers cut on the small radio and a Black Sabbath song came through the speakers.

"Tykisha, none of those facts on Kalana Watson are admissible in court." He busied himself walking over to the board. Rodgers wrote Icy Bezel's name on the board before he continued speaking.

"I obtained it when that psychopath was in the nuthouse heavily medicated." Rodgers made direct eye contact with Kish, emphasizing HEAVILY MEDICATED.

"You gave her SODIUM AMYTAL!" Kish was wide eyed in disbelief. Never in a million years would she have thought that her Uncle G, highly decorated Special Agent George Rodgers would intentionally break the law.

"We're easily talking the Death Penalty on this crazy broad!" Rodgers said with a little chuckle. "One way or another these homicides gonna stick!"

At that very point Kish lost all respect for her mentor and the man she called uncle and looked up to. Her whole aspect on law enforcement at that time shifted. Unveiled was the thought that everyone is corrupt and Kish's actions, conflictions, and bond towards the family felt justified. *"Aha!"* Kish thought.

Every chair in Ms. Benita's Nu Look beauty salon was filled on Friday afternoon. Beyoncé singing fiercely through the salons surround sound could be heard under the laughter and all the conversations. The bells on the door ringing indicated a new patron. The noise and all the voices in the establishment died down in a trickle effect once every eye in the place looking directly or side eyed got a glimpse of Lana.

She walked tall and proud; her strides were like a giraffe. She could pass for an R&B pop star, as well as a runway model or famous celebrity socialite. The sophisticated yet sensually dressed Lana wore a Paco heel. The white boots matched her sleek, white pea coat by MK. It came down hugging the top of Lana's thick thighs. A MK white clutch, along with a pair of white seventies-styled glasses by MK as well, was only half of her flawless appearance. The other half was completed and complimented by the diamonds and gold jewelry. Not gaudy or big but small and significant. Her earrings, watch, and bracelets each twinkled and danced to all the onlookers under the shops fluorescent lights.

NeNe admired the stunning woman that had just walked through the doors of the beauty shop. Her back was to Lana but NeNe watched her from the mirrors on the wall she was facing.

"Mmm mmm mmm!" NeNe said just loud enough for her hair stylist to hear.

"Girl I thought you had a man now and was strictly dickly," the girl styling NeNe's hair said to her.

NeNe replied, "A fine thing like that will make any bitch backslide."

NeNe wasn't considered pretty by anyone, maybe cute at best. Her slim waist and bubble butt were the assets she held that stopped men in their tracks. The blond sew-in that the beautician was applying to NeNe's head, was a stark contrast to her dark chocolate skin tone.

For the next two hours, NeNe made it obvious to Lana by the frequent glances and brief smiles that she was feeling her. Lana had spotted her target as soon as she walked in the shop.

She knew that NeNe came to Ms. Benita's every other Friday. That information was courtesy of X's longtime friend, Ms. Benita. She was in the club the night Coco and his goons came there asking for X just before they shot up the place.

When NeNe was finished getting her hair done she walked over to Lana who was getting her nails filled. "How you doing gorgeous?" NeNe asked looking down at the seated Lana's breast that were busting out of her blouse.

Lana looked up giving NeNe a mischievous smile, "Hello."

In Wilmington, Delaware, X was at a meeting he had arranged with Fame, one half of the once murderous Dominican twins. X walked beside Fame who was being pushed in a wheelchair through the vendors of Market Street Mall. Almost a year ago, Fame and his now deceased brother Money, were ordered to kill X by their boss El OSO. Due to an unexpected change of events X ended up saving Fame's life. It was only because of that that Fame had agreed to this meeting. True to his name, everything about Fame, his attitude and style of clothes screamed out famous, even though he was in therapy learning to walk again.

"What's on your mind Cabron?" The dark-skinned Dominican being pushed in a wheelchair asked X before he continued, "this is the first and last time I agree to meet up with you, this is still El OSO's city."

X nodded in agreement then spoke. "That's part of the reason I'm up here." X paused to look at the chubby older Dominican clad from head to toe in Versace that was pushing Fame's wheelchair.

"He's cool," Fame said seeing X's reluctant look, "this is my uncle

Floco, I trust him with my Life!"

X grinned, "I hope so because I'm bout to tell you something mind blowing!" X stopped talking only to inhale the blunt smoke. "But first before I give you this info." X passed the blunt to Fame. "Do you have what I asked for?"

Fame spoke to his Uncle in Spanish. Floco's two small Cuban Link chains weighed down each by diamond encrusted Jesus pieces dangled as he bent over to hear Fame who spoke to him rapidly just above a whisper. With a thick Spanish accent Floco described Evita's whereabouts.

"She's in beautiful Constanza, the coldest town in Dominican Republic. She lives in a Ranch home on their grandfather's apple and peach orchid. Cabron, don't be fooled by the serene display. There are henchmen and bodyguards all over so it will not be a simple task to extract your love."

"Gracious," X said to Fame's uncle Floco shaking the man's hand.

He knew the elder Dominican could have refused to reveal Evita's location, and Fame couldn't make him. Floco stopped pushing the wheelchair and motioned with his hand for X to pass the blunt. He didn't continue to push the chair. He and Fame both stood motionless staring at X, waiting…X got the cue.

"O, y'all waiting on me?" he asked with a sly smile, "okay, you all know that my cousin Lana took out your beloved boss Jesus and his top enforcer Pepe…but let me tell you where the order came down from…"

In the mist of the crowded vender filled Market street, Fame and Floco's undivided attention was on X's every word.

"El OSO killed his brother. He was tired of sharing the helm of the

Cartel. He wanted the sole and undisputed title of top Dominican Don!"

Fame was speechless, while his loyal Uncle who had served in the Cartel since El OSO and Jesus' father started it almost twenty years ago was fuming.

"Muthafuck'n haza!"

Before X left Fame and his uncle he remembered one thing. "Fame, if you see to Evita before me, tell her come to the Clara Lee at the marina down Seaford!"

Lana played hard to get for close to an hour before she gave in to NeNe's sexual advances. NeNe didn't waist anytime getting Lana into her Acura coop.

"I'll bring you back to your ride tonight or morning," NeNe said to Lana shrugging.

Just before arriving to her house in Middletown, Delaware, NeNe called Coco.

"Hello, Babe. You should come on home. I have a sweet juicy treat for us both to share." NeNe shifted her phone so Coco could see Lana in the passenger seat.

Lana leaned in close to NeNe and placed a slow gentle kiss on her cheek, leaving red lipstick. "I'm bout to take your girl."

Coco's diamond's and gold gleamed even through the phones camera as he smiled. "Say Word? Don't nuttin go down without me, da HNIC!"

"Well what the fuck you waiting on!" Lana quipped sticking out her tongue.

Fifteen minutes later after their video call with Coco, Lana was being led through the door of NeNe's townhouse. Lana's eyes scoured her surroundings as NeNe led her by the hand upstairs, into her bedroom. Lana's mind raced, she felt giddy and anxious inside. She knew it was only a matter of time before Coco arrived. Lana's body tingled and a warm calm rushed over her. She was a professional in her element, like a carpenter with wood or a mason with stone. Lana didn't freeze up from her adrenaline rush she rode it.

"X, I'm at NeNe's house waiting on the NY dude, Coco! Get here ASAP! Middletown 106 Royle Courts!" Lana was hitting SEND when NeNe called for her from the shower.

"Hey Sexy, come on in here!" NeNe grinned like a Cheshire cat when Lana snatched back the shower curtain, revealing her exquisite body.

NeNe looked at Lana from head to toes greedily. Lana waited for NeNe's eyes to return back up to her face before she smiled and covered he mouth. Lana expelled a razor from her lips as smooth as an ATM spitting out bills.

NeNe's throat was slit before her smile vanished then dread and panic filled her eyes. Blood squirted and poured out of NeNe's neck as she slipped and fell back, pulling down the shower curtain. The tiled wall was splattered with blood as the shower water continued to pelt down on NeNe. Red blood and water ran down the drain.

Lana stood naked not moving a muscle, watching the life seep from NeNe's eyes. Her phone ringing in the bedroom broke her trance. Lana ran into the room and answered it.

"Come open the door, Cuz." Without hesitation Lana ran downstairs to open the door.

When X stepped in, he shielded his face from Lana's nakedness.

"GIRL, put some fuckin' clothes on!" X spat.

He waited at the bottom of the stairs until Lana went up and covered herself with one of NeNe's robes.

"Come on up, Cuz!" she yelled.

As soon as X walked into the bedroom, he questioned Lana.

"Where's the broad?"

Lana pointed to the bathroom inside the bedroom. X peeped his head in there and shook his head sadly at the corpse in the tub. X knew he was the one solely responsible for Lana's transformation and blood thirst. Before he could ask why, they both heard the door open downstairs.

Brandishing a colt 45 revolver tucked under his Fly Legend Polo shirt, X motioned to Lana to get on the bed while he backed into the bathroom. X shut the door behind him, cut the shower back on and listened intently.

Coco stopped at the door to the bedroom, the cracked door creaked as he pushed it all the way open. The display he saw dissolved any suspicions he may have had on an ambush. Walking into the bedroom he placed his roscoe on top of the dresser, then sat on the edge of the bed, watching Lana masturbate.

Between moans and panting Lana manage to say, "NeNe's taking a shower."

But Coco's mind wasn't on the whereabouts of NeNe. His rod grew harder by the second as Lana's juices glistened on her hand and stained the purple sheets. Coco couldn't resist the beautiful sight and he placed his face between Lana's soft legs. Before Lana could push his head away she felt Coco's soft but stiff tongue.

"HMMMM!" she moaned.

X had his ear to the bathroom door and couldn't believe what was going on, he snatched the door open. Grabbing Coco by the back of his neck, X stuck the revolver to his temple.

"Get yo dumb ass up!" X smacked Coco with the side of the pistol creating a gash instantly. Coco's lips were glazed over as they opened and closed trying to find words but nothing came out.

"Let me kill 'em," Lana said as she started dressing.

"Unbelievable!" X thought to himself.

Coco finally got his wits together enough to speak. "Who the fuck sent YOU! Country Boy you robbing ME..." Coco laid still in the floor with his hands up, his eyes never leaving X's eyes. He continued, "you signing your own Death Certificate!"

Lana now fully dressed stood beside X, who held his 45-barrel gun steady on the prone but defiant Coco. Putting on her earrings Lana questioned.

"Who tha fuck you been looking for nigga?" After she placed on her earrings Lana stepped around Coco, still questioning. "Who the fuck is you?" Lana raised her foot and stomped down hard on Coco's face. "Nobody gave you permission to taste my pussy!"

With X's pistol trained on him Coco didn't dare go on the offense. "You X?" Coco asked knowing the answer, "gotta give you props Country Boy," Coco said with a bloody grin, "you got the drop on me. Whatcha you gon, do God?"

X motioned with his free had. "Get up. We not gonna kill you."

"WHAT!" Lana spat.

She back stepped to the dresser that Coco's pistol laid on. Lana picked up the pistol and pointed it at the now standing Coco.

"HOOO!" Coco said ducking Lana's aim.

Lana continued, "He bought goons and guns to the party…looking to KILL you, Cuz!"

X sighed, frustrated at the blood thirsty Lana. "Put the gun down Lana, we not gonna send 'em to hell yet. I don't think the God wanted to kill, he wanted to do business. Right?"

He then turned back to Coco who was nodding his head up and down.

"Hell yeah!" The gears in X's head were turning as soon as he laid eyes on Coco and heard him speak.

"Where you from?" X questioned?

"Brooklyn!" Coco said confidently.

"No," X said, "I'm talking bout your homeland."

Coco responded, "I'm Puerto Rican." X shook his head.

"We gonna do business. Put your number in this phone." X handed Coco a flip phone while Coco punched his name and number into the flip, X continued speaking, "but for shooting up my coming home party, we taking everything...and for your sake I hope you holding some major paper AND or big work."

Coco shook his head disgusted at himself for getting caught slipping but he did have his life.

X continued, "Because my Cuz as you can see, just wants any excuse to kill you. BREAK BREAD NEW YORK CITY!"

CHAPTER 6

Black Duck

Lavender Smith AKA Icy Bezel's day began with so much promise. Friday landed on the first of month. So not only would junkies and crack heads be spending their paychecks, SSI and disability checks came out as well today. At 6 a.m. Icy Bezel wearing an orange hard hat and a reflective vest was en route, in an old red Ford Ranger to the Black House meeting Kish. Icy Bezel always wore a work disguise when he was riding dirty. His only companion was a black Desert Eagle semi-automatic pistol that he called Black Duck, laying on the passenger's seat.

The last five kilos of coke that the Family had jacked from the Mexican were in a black duffel bag in the Ford's truck bed. It was dawn and the mist was thick when Icy Bezel met up with Kish in The Roc at the Black House. Icy Bezel stepped out of the truck into the light fog. He inhaled and exhaled deeply.

"That good 'ol country air!" Icy Bezel said to Kish who was already outside her car and waiting by the back door.

"Boy this shit stinks out here!" The chicken manure that the farmers used as fertilizer was all that could be smelled.

Icy Bezel laughed as he unlocked the door to the small house. He let Kish go in before him. Stepping into the house after her, he paused just before he closed the door. He stuck his head back outside, looking over the back yard and into the woods.

"That's weird," Icy Bezel said quietly.

"What?" Kish said from in the kitchen.

"Nothing," Icy Bezel said turning to join her inside closing the door.

The Black House wasn't black actually, just its windows were. Icy Bezel had put midnight black tint on all of the windows of the house. It prevented people from the outside to see not even a sliver of light, if they tried looking into the house.

Icy Bezel carried the two duffel bags full of work and Kish had two Walmart bags filled with boxes of baking soda.

"You ready to get busy, Homegirl?" Icy Bezel said cutting on the lights. He tried to harmonize like Bone Thugs. "Its tha first of the month. Cash yo checks and come on!"

Kish laughed, "You sound good too. But don't quit your day job." Laughing as she pulled the pyrex from the cupboard.

"Let's get this money!" Kish said as she laid different items out on the square fold up table. Scale, Arm & Hammer, sandwich bags and lastly her chrome .380 caliber pistol. Icy Bezel pulled one key from the duffle bag and placed it on the table.

"You did good last time you chefed up, go ahead and do your thang," Icy Bezel said pointing to the kilo then sitting in one of the two chairs at the table.

"What you think I was getting all the shit ready for? Imma cook this shit up...drop it down to the oils," Kish said giving Icy Bezel a playful smirk.

She was at the table braking ice from ice trays filling up a basin. Icy Bezel didn't look up from the chess game he was playing on his iPhone.

He only said, "Hug huh."

Kish continued, "I got THIS, you just cut some sounds on for me."

Icy Bezel's head popped up. "What you say?"

Kish was hitting the brick of cocaine with a hammer now as she stopped and answered, feigning being annoyed.

"Some SOUNDS! You know some MUSIC!" Kish said slowly.

It wasn't until Icy Bezel witnessed Kish blowing out the Mexicans brains that he started to trust her and accept Kish as Family. Each day that passed was a blessing to him. He was well aware that he had went too far and stayed too long in the game. Icy Bezel had his future planned. He would relocate to Cali...

"Southern Cali invest in movies and wine," he thought to himself.

They were both his passions throughout all the drug dealing and occasional killings. Bezel felt the weight of the paranoia and anxiety that comes with being in the underworld leaving from his shoulders, as he was ever so close. Closer to getting his million and disappearing from this hellish reality he had known all his life. Times had definitely changed. The once "easy streets" for a hustler was a thing of the past. With pros that gained fast money in large denomination had but all then dried up and turned sour. Those glory days of making money, hand over fist without any repercussion, had been replaced by death or football numbers by the judge. Icy Bezel noticed himself smiling more and having less uneasiness, like his usual self, as the days grew closer for MZ Rae to deliver. He welcomed a new life free of the threat of getting killed in a shootout or going to jail with open arms. The twenty bricks they had taken from the Cholo was The Family's last Act before their grand finale.

"Off these last five birds and get my million then I'm through! With my mill and the percentage from all the bricks...I'll be GOOD."

This sentence was on repeat in Icy Bezel's mind. His repetitive objective was interrupted and came to a halt when he heard the word SOUNDS from Kish.

"Something don't feel right!" Icy said to himself.

He couldn't put his finger on it when he had paused at the back door and looked into the woods before entering the house.

"SOUNDS!" It hit him when he said the word in his head. "Sounds!" He thought about what he heard when he got out his truck up until he walked into the house.

"Come to think of it," he said to himself, *"there wasn't any of the sounds normally heard in the country in the morning!"*

Country mornings were always full of different noises and sounds. Roosters cock-o-doodling, dogs barking, and birds chirping and singing are apparent on any given country morning. It only took seconds for all these thoughts to come across Icy Bezel's mind.

Kish repeated, "Are you gonna cut some music on or what?"

Before Icy Bezel could react to his "spidey sense" there was a knock at the door.

"Fiends biting all ready," Kish said grabbing and cocking her .380 that laid next to a wad of rubber bands and a T. Jones money counter.

"Who is it?" Icy Bezel's voice said sharply.

"It's ya boy," a voice responded back.

The tone of the voice wasn't aggressive or passive. Nor was it soft or hard. The voice was neutral and lacking all emotion, nondescript and unrecognizable. Icy Bezel instinctively reached for Black Duck that was tucked normally on his waistline but came up empty.

"Damn!" He remembered he left the pistol on the seat in the truck.

"Hold up!" Icy Bezel yelled to Kish who was unlocking the dead bolt.

"It's a lick," Kish said opening the door. Before she could turn the knob the door was knocked back into her, forcefully coming off its hinges.

"FBI! MUTHAFUCA!"

Two linebacker-sized White men bust through the door, dropping their brown battering ram that read Ghetto Blaster down its side. Kish flew into the table crashing through it down to the flora linoleum floor.

Icy Bezel was busy trying to get the bricks. He had grabbed the one from the table just before Kish came crashing through it. As he picked up the duffle from the floor and gave an about face jetting through the living room he heard two shots. He seen Kish to his left through his peripheral vision firing her pistol from the same place she'd landed in the floor.

"Come on Girl!" Icy Bezel hollered waving to Kish to follow.

He had seen Kish drop one of the cops that barged through the door.

"Fuck! I'm hit!" Agent Russell shouted crumbling to the floor.

Return fire came back rapidly in spurts.

"PATTTDD, PRARTTDD!"

Icy Bezel dove behind an old piano in the living room. A broken tune was played when bullets ripped through the organ hitting keys. Icy bezel only lay down flat and still for a second. Looking back, he jumped to his feet from his off of knees, Icy Bezel watched as Kish took two shots in the chest.

She screamed out in pain, "GO!"

Kish howled in agony to Icy Bezel while one of the numerous men in black fatigue kicked the pistol from her hands. Trying to get away was his number one priority. "Get away and stash this shit somewhere!"

He knew he didn't have time to hit the bathroom to flush it. They were already in the house. Icy Bezel knew that in any raid that "dem boyz" is at the front door to. He was focused on getting to a bedroom to jump out of one of the windows and double time it to the woods. Three agents in the same black fatigues bust through the front door simultaneously, while the others knocked down the back door, intercepted Icy Bezel.

Icy Bezel held his hands up as the men surrounded him. One of the agents snatched the duffle bag from Icy Bezel's hand, while another gave him a brutal blow from the butt of his assault rifle.

"Jackpot!" Icy Bezel heard one of the agents say as he was being aggressively hand cuffed and frisked.

Blood poured from a gash on the side of his head and ran down into his eyes. He was read his Miranda Rights as he was hoisted to his feet and led back through the kitchen. Icy Bezel seen one of the agents placing a white sheet over Kish and another one was administering CPR to the agent Kish had shot.

"Fuck!" Icy Bezel spat as he was partially dragged and carried out of the house by two agents.

Afterwards, Icy Bezel was thrown into the back of black Suburban and hauled off to the nearest local precinct. When the truck was heard being gunned from the house, Kish and the Agent she'd shot both raised up. She sat up removing the white sheet. Agent Rodgers got to his feet first before Kish. He had given Kish the order that this was her last assignment on this case a day before.

"Agent Tykisha Moore, you've gathered enough substantial evidence on the Diamond State Mob," Agent Rodgers said to Kish, "you've done your duty. Because of you they'll go down for murder one and using a criminal enterprise to fuel legitimate businesses."

Kish's stomach flipped as Agent Rodgers delivered her last orders on this mission.

"I'm not ready to abandon the Family!" Kish said to herself.

Just as the feeling was voiced in her subconscious, Kish reprimanded herself. *"Did you just hear what you said? You've got a job to do! They are not my Family!"* she stilled herself.

"Imma even let you go out with a BANG!" Agent Rodgers said as he handed her the chrome .380 filled with blanks.

The Don received the call in the middle of a game of Capicu with his elderly uncle. "Boss…I found him…"

Francisco Ramirez gave no reply, he just listened to one of his trusted soldiers, Hector, speak of his only nephew Ricardo.

"They desecrated his body…"

Don Ramirez deep baritone voice rumbled as he spat in a heavy Spanish accent.

"What did they do?!" Hector apprehensively answered his boss.

"They chopped him up and put his body parts in our chicken houses. They picked him clean."

It had been two weeks since Hector had seen Ricardo. He had searched every inch of the house and property. Hector and the Don were already thinking the worst after a week had past. After no luck looking for Ricardo in the horse stables Hector checked the land for any signs of a shallow grave. The five chicken houses were the last places one would think to look, and just like anyone else Hector checked them last. While walking through the last of the chicken houses when he was just about to abandon his search he noticed that the majority of the birds were gathered to the rear. It was hard to see the floor in the dim and dusty amber lit room. The birds scattered as he got closer, revealing a picked rib cage and carcass.

The sight made Hector back paddle. He felt his foot kick something and when he looked down, it was a skull. It was unmistakably Ricardo's head. Even though his eyes were gone and most of the skin and meat were missing as well Ricardo's long hair was a dead giveaway.

Don Francisco said nothing more he just pressed END on the flip phone. He was well aware that Ricardo was in bed with the FEDS. Francisco didn't know that his nephew was literally in bed with one of them but it wasn't hard for him to come to the conclusion that "gringos" had something to do with Ricardo's death.

"Fucking gringo pigs!" Francisco said spitting on the ground.

The accord he had set with FBI agent Rodgers had ran smooth for over two years. Agent Rodgers made sure Francisco's mules arrived safely with his drugs to the Eastern Shore once a month. In return Francisco had his men fulfill various requests from the FEDS. From muscling and extorting, to at times murdering the people that kept on slipping from the tentacles of prosecution or that had gotten too big for the judicial system.

A few pedophiles had been acquitted, multiple times in the court of law but weeks later were found dead with their penis' in their mouths. Francisco especially enjoyed bringing justice to those dogs. As long as the FED'S demands were being met the drugs flowed freely from Mexico to Delaware, Maryland, and Virginia like clockwork.

Don Francisco pulled out another flip phone and dialed the only number in it. He paced back and forth on the porch of his villa.

"Cabron, mi brothers son is dead! Is this how you treat your amigos?"

CHAPTER 7

Aunt Mary's

In Wilmington, Delaware, in front of a Westside project building, Isis and O.G. sat on a park bench. Amongst all of the hustle and bustle of any city block in the U.S., people came and went in and out of the stores. O.G. and Isis' focus were only on two people on the crowded block. They smoked a blunt while they were watching the coke they had gotten for free turn into dollars.

O.G.'s cousin Bump said they could off the work on his block for a small fee. Isis and O.G. witnessed Bump and his young boys operate like a well-oiled machine. There were no hand-to-hands made outside, only inside the project halls. Outside the fiends gave Bump the money. After the fiends passed off the cash, they were allowed to enter the apartment. When they received their drugs from Bump's youngin' the fiends kept going, exiting out the back door.

Bump's fee for letting them sell their coke was that they give him a brick when they were done and that he would be the one to sell their work. O.G. and Isis agreed both parties would benefit. The Family was getting the price they wanted plus, getting the product off without taking the risk. All they had to do was sit back, chill then collect.

They enjoyed the change of scenery from the country. In southern Delaware where they were from, this locking down of blocks and buildings was a thing of the past. They operated on back roads and country holes deep in the woods. Isis just loved she could wear some nice clothes and shoes without having to walk in dirt. Her basic B-girl look still had sass causing a few of the "up top boyz" as Isis called them to approach and compliment. Brandon Maxwell jeans accented the petite Isis' hips, thighs and butt. Her white blouse that hung loosely around her neck, letting a small necklace be seen stopping at her bosoms, matched her heels. White Vince Camuto heels exposed Isis' perfectly pedicured toes and honey tanned feet. Isis had blonde highlights throughout her short Halle Berry style haircut. Her chinky eyes disappeared as smoke rushed from her mouth and nose while she laughed and coughed.

"What you mean the boys wouldn't know what to do with me?" she asked O.G. referring to the statement he said after the last "up top boy" stopped to talk to Isis.

"You'll run all over these cats. With that art of seduction type shit you and Lana study," O.G. continued after he took the blunt that Isis passed, "then you'll fuck around and rob him."

Isis' phone rang as they both laughed.

"Hello…Hello?" Not being able to understand what was being said on the other end. It was Lana, she was sobbing uncontrollably.

"Kish is DEAD!" Isis heard crystal clear in Lana's inaudible speech. Isis put her on speaker phone, her and O.G. listened as Lana told Icy Bezel and Kish's fates. In between sniffling and crying Lana continued, "family meeting tomorrow in Milford at Aunt Mary's…Isis I love you. No matter what we went through…"

Isis interjected wiping a tear from her eye, "I know Lana. I love you too and feel you 100%! See you tomorrow."

Aunt Mary closed the doors of her soul food restaurant to the public for the Family meeting. Aunt Mary and her niece were the only other people, besides the Family in the building. They were the only staff. Like every Family meeting, everyone got a turn to speak. Sista Vic spoke first between a forkful of a Caesar salad.

"They got Lavender with five whole chickens. They got the child's bail up to a million dollars!" she said washing her salad down with an Arnold Palmer.

She shook her head and sighed heavily, "Lavender told me he seen Kish get killed with his own two eyes. The hospital and the police said she's deceased but shipped her body to her nearest relative."

Sista Vic scanned her Family, every one of them she loved as her children. Looking up and into the eyes of X, Lana, Kush, O.G. and Isis. She lowered her voice to a whisper.

"No one would tell me who the relative was or where they were sending the girl." Kush and X exchanged brief eye contact. "Can you believe that?" Sista Vic's voice faded off into silence at noticing the look Kush and X shared.

She sat without saying another word, waiting for an explanation from X and Kush.

Finally Kush spoke up, "The Family's been infiltrated by an undercover federal agent."

Lana, Sista Vic, and Isis all gasped in shock and horror. O.G. dropped his head. Everyone knew what that met, that jail time was looming. Kush was bombarded with questions from all the Family members except X.

Lana's voice carried over everyone's, "How long have you known about this? Here we go on this secretive bullshit!"

X knew if the Family didn't trust one another they all could kiss their millions goodbye and their freedom.

"No!" X intervened.

"We just was trying to figure out who it was." Now it was Isis turn.

"Trying to figure OUT, who you thought it was?" Isis snapped her neck and rolled her eyes, "so you think Kish is an alphabet boy?"

O.G. shook his head while peeling and eating shrimp. "I know something wasn't right with that broad!"

"Shut up!" Isis told him.

"You shut up bitch!" O.G. responded, "you just mad cause that was your homegirl."

Kush calmed them down. "Alright now y'all. If Kish is the Feds we in trouble."

Everyone shook their heads in agreement as Kush continued, "we gonna have to get this money and bounce. Get the fuck outta the country!"

X asked Lana, "Have you talked to MZ Rae?"

"Yes, I talked to her today," Lana said, "she's in the Caymans now. The bank can make her wait up to two weeks to withdrawal that amount of cash."

"Damn!" Isis said.

"NO!" Kush said, "that might be a good thing."

"What you talking bout?" X asked.

Kush stood up and began to pace the restaurant while he thought, *"Maybe it'll be best if all of us made the trip down to the Caymans."* He looked up to see their reactions.

They were all listening. "Considering our circumstances," Kush continued, "we don't know what the FEDS or state boys got on us but waiting until they come ain't an option for me!"

The Family took a few moments pondering on what Kush was saying. It was either stay and wait for an indictment from the feds or go on the run abroad. Being absconded with a half a mill or more sounded a lot better than a cold cell for a decade. One by one they all agreed to go down to the Cayman Islands except X.

"I gotta go to DR."

Isis smacked her lips knowing the reason why X was going to Dominican. "Evita!" Isis missed the relationship her and X once had. He was her mentor, her first and only love. X gave Isis a bone chilling icy look before turning to speak to the Family as a whole.

"I've got to handle my BI; I got a little baby girl down there…"

O.G. interjected, "I'll go with you."

"No!" X shot back, "I gotta do this on my own. Y'all just get down there to safety." X smiled as he continued, "and have my pension and retirement money ready for me."

Everyone laughed around the two tables that had been joined together to accommodate the Family. Their pot of gold was in sight. It wasn't at the end of a rainbow, but more like a bumpy and turbulent rollercoaster ride full ups and downs. For a brief moment each one of the Family members minds traveled millions of miles away. They all visualized different scenes of themselves living carefree and wealthy.

Kush pictured himself on the island of Ko Phi Phi Leh with two beautiful Thai women, reclining back on the beach with limestone hills in the backdrops. He had always wanted to go there since he had seen the movie The Beach. O.G. daydreamed of being in Monaco at the Formula 1

Grand Prix race. He could already feel the gust of wind through his white linen shorts and shirt as the cars made their circuit. Isis saw herself being landed by helicopter on the Burj al Arab hotel's helipad. The hem from her stunning off-shoulder evening gown blew as the helicopter took off leaving her star struck at the breathtaking view of Dubai.

Sista Vic even dared to dream with her big payoff so close. Her eyes twinkled with the thought of her buying an estate in her mother's homeland of Belize. She had never been there before but from the vivid stories of the serene and picturesque landscapes that her mother described during her childhood, Sista Vic always knew that was the place for her. Their daydreams were interrupted by Lana.

"Wait a minute! Didn't y'all say Kish killed that La EME Cholo?"

"YEAHHHH!" Everyone said in unison.

Isis questioned, "How does a federal justify killing for The Family? How do we know for sure that Kish was the mole?"

She looked at everyone around the tables. "I'd hate it to come to pass that Kish was official and someone in HERE is a Federal fucking agent!"

X banged on the table with his fist. "That bitch is the cops! Kish the last one we brought into the Family!" X paused while he split a dutchie. He put the blunt guts in his finished plate of ox tail, rice and cabbage. "Plus, all of us at this table has known each other for over ten years."

Isis snaked her head and neck as she sat up in the chair. "We all didn't know Lana until a couple years ago…could be her!" Isis said pointing to Lana.

"Fuck you bitch!" Lana said pointing back at Isis. "I ain't no damn cop and you better leave me the fuck alone!" Lana's reserved demeanor grew hostile within seconds. Isis knew well the wildness that filled Lana's eyes at this moment.

X lit the fat blunt he had rolled. He shook his head as he inhaled and exhaled. "Everyone in here KNOWS Lana ain't the Jake!"

After the meeting was over X pulled Kush to the side out of earshot from the rest of The Family.

"Bro, keep an eye on Lana until she gets on that plane to the Caymans."

Kush smiled, saying, "She's a big girl, Queen B can hold her own, X."

X looked Kush in the eyes seriously. "I don't think she taking her medication. I'm not worried about someone hurting her, I'm worried bout her hurting herself and whoever else!"

The old friends shook hands and embraced.

"I got you dog," Kush said, "go get your baby girl and Evita. I'll be waiting in paradise with a fat blunt and a cool mill! Family Love!"

CHAPTER 8

Pretty Eyes

Gerald gritted his teeth, clenching his jaws as he watched Kalana exchange hugs and say goodbyes to some people in front of a restaurant. He had to admit to himself that Kalana was gorgeous.

"Bitch!" Gerald spat as he followed Lana to her car with his eyes through binoculars.

He snatched his brother's Lexus into drive and pulled off after Lana's Audi A8. Gerald thought of how close he had gotten to her the night before at the Dover casino. Just thinking of the encounter made him smell her fragrance.

"Excuse me, I just wanted to tell you that you're a beautiful young lady. Feels like your radiating with sunshine and positivity."

Lana was at roulette table. She hadn't taken her medication since she'd been home from the psych ward. Her thoughts were all over the place and most of her actions were impulsive. Lana's white blouse peaked out from the soft pink thin trench coat by Roman's. The lightweight jacket's label was flourished down to the cinched belt, tied loosely around Lana's small waist. Her curves showed even conservatively dressed. Form fitting white pants could be seen starting at the top of her thigh down to her lower calf. Gold Isabel Marant heels matched Lana's gold earrings, necklace, rings and bracelets. Lana's natural beauty and attraction left Gerald speechless when she turned to him smiling.

"I wonder how many young ladies you've said that to tonight."

The photos Gerald had of Lana didn't do her any justice. In person, she was stunning but Gerald told himself he couldn't forget that she's still a cold-blooded killer. He stuttered to get his next words out.

"Y-y-y-you're the only women in here worthy of my time." Gerald held up his hands. "I'm sorry I was just giving a Black woman a compliment. Your beauty is appreciated." He pointed to the ball that had stopped on 42 BLACK.

"You've won!"

Lana's attention was on Gerald's pretty eyes, "Oh!" Lana said with an innocent adolescent smile.

As she reached for her chips, Gerald noticed that she had a finger missing. They shared a few drinks at the bar after Lana cashed in her chips. It took all of Gerald's inner strength not to wrap his hands around the pretty Lana's neck and strangle her to death that night. The two exchanged numbers and promised to meet up again soon. Gerald promised himself that once he got her in an intimate setting that he would introduce himself and kill her slowly.

"Today's the day Kalana Watson," Gerald said as he tailed Lana on the busy Route 1-13 Highway.

Michel Camilo's piano tunes floated like butterflies out of the villa's open windows. The music reflected the mood of the typical perfect Caribbean mid-day. Soft faint moans peaked over the music's slow melody. The elated whines had their very own rhythm.

"Vita. Mama...Mu caliente!"

Evita cooed, "Papiii!"

Evita's skin tone was a rich vibrant ocher in color. It glistened from perspiration, laying down the hair on her arms. Evita's long, silky black hair was being pulled from the back, forcing her closed eyes to face the ceiling. The doggie style back shots were soft and hard. Evita could feel one of her soft butt cheeks being palmed and spread open, as she was getting thrusted into, slow and deep. A light breeze blew the silk drapes from the canopy styled bed over the two lovers. The strokes got faster deeper and more intense. Sounds of pleasure escaped both of the lover's mouths.

"I love you Vita!" Evita heard.

Feeling blissful, her senses disregarded the heavy accent. Evita heard what she wanted to hear, which was X's distinctive baritone.

As she climaxed, "Yusef" trembled from her lips in a whisper.

"Mama…Dada." A small voice coming from the next room was heard by the collapsed and panting couple.

"Coming, Daddy's Little Princes!"

Evita's eyes popped opened as the man jumped from the bed. He slipped on some shorts before hurriedly walking out of the room. Evita pouted; her fantasy had vanished when her eyes opened. Every time she had ever had sex with Hector, Evita envisioned X's powerful physique. She covered herself with a silk sheet as Hector walked back into the bedroom carrying a little girl. He talked to the baby as he held her up to the high ceiling.

"Look at Daddy' baby girl!"

Evita smiled at hearing the giggles of her daughter. There still was sadness in her heart. Evita yearned for her soul mate's touch or even just his reassuring presence.

"Until we meet again in the next life," Evita said to herself.

Ximena's real father, Yusef Watson aka X, Evita presumed was dead. The last time Evita had seen X he was held at gunpoint, moments away from being executed. That was nine months ago. Her brother El OSO forced her to come back to their homeland of the Dominican Republic. El OSO arranged the merging of their and the Renoso family with the engagement and marriage of Evita to Hector.

Hector Renoso came from a prominent and wealthy family that traced its roots back to the Maroons of the island. His great-grandfather not only became rich, growing various fruit he had passed down a fortune from the sugar cane industry. Hector and his family owned DR Airlines, the most reliable airlines of the Caribbean.

The families' merger was similar to two fortune five hundred companies merging together. Hector would ensure that El OSO's drugs would make it to the northeast of the United States. Evita reasoned that this was the best situation for her daughter and family, considering her true love was gone. Her own brother, El OSO, killed him. Hector was a great man and father. Evita felt that she should be grateful that a wealthy good man thinks that he fathered her child and wanted to marry her. But she wasn't. Evita felt a huge void and her secret weighed heavy on her conscience, even more when she witnessed Hector and Ximena interacting.

CHAPTER 9

Dear Momma

Lana left Aunt Mary's Soul Food with her mind racing and emotions in limbo.

"Kish is dead…I brought her into this Family. It's my fault. I'm responsible!" Lana became frantic, "gotta get some clothes, hit the airport. Which airport? BWI? Dulles? Ronald Reagan? NY? Shit, I gotta tell my mother!"

Lana's phone rang as she was stopped at a red light digging in her console, searching for her G-pin. Yo Gotti's *"My O.G."* song played as the ringtone.

"Kush! I'll call you back!" Lana said out loud. Her mind was only on finding the electronic pin that held honey flavored THC oil. "Got you!" Lana yelled.

She stuck the tip of the device into her mouth and inhaled while pressing a button on the side of it. Lana blew out a puff of smoke from the honey infused potion. She busted a right on Harrington-Milford road, headed to her mother's house. The cannabis pin relaxed Lana. The jumbled-up thoughts that bombarded her brain minutes ago became manageable now. Sort of like 10 people all trying to get in a small door versus those same ten people walking into the door in a single file line. Lana turned Cardi B on and took another puff from the pin as she went over her game plan.

"Imma go to Mom's, say goodbye to her, get some cash and a couple outfits then hit the airport." The effects from G pin settled Lana's anxiety. She could feel the tingly, calming sensation engulfing and spreading throughout her body.

"Gotta call MZ Rae to tell her that plans have changed. That we flying down and that Kish is dead." Lana felt sorrow for only a few as she pushed Kish's face out of mind. She forced herself to think about the good times ahead abroad and with her Family. Lana shook her head and grooved her body to Cardi B.

"Yeah!" she said to herself while bopping to the beat, "That's it! Then get the bag and island hop for a few years bitch!" Lana busted out laughing.

The Audi's V8 engine hemmed as Lana gunned it through the long country back roads. The everyday colors of the country were vivid under the bright sun and blue skies.

Lana thought, *"A Perfect Day for a new life."*

Gerald had to fall back about a mile from Lana as he continued his stealthy pursuit onto the country roads where traffic was sparse. He drove past endless miles of cornfields, chicken houses and trees. Kalana was so far ahead of Gerald that he thought he had lost sight of the German made car. After rounding two big curves, the road straightened out and Gerald got a glimpse for two seconds of the tail end of the black sedan about a quarter of a mile ahead. He drove past the sprawling multi-acre property Kalana had turned into. The long driveway sat in between two white fences that spanned hundreds of yards in both directions. Gerald saw a few horses inside the white fences and also observed a dog heading to Kalana's car. He drove until the white fence met a huge cornfield. Gerald pulled the Lexus into a farmers trail that cut through the cornstalks. He stopped the car about a half a mile into the field. He chambered a bullet then proceeded to trek between the rows of corn toward the farmhouse. Gerald reasoned he would walk until he reached the fence then follow it to the property's rear. After peeping out the scene and its surroundings from back there he would advance cautiously.

"But first gotta handle this fucking dog!"

Lana exhaled and relaxed at just the sight of the blue ranch home. X had bought it for her after what the Virginia police dubbed "The Chesapeake Massacre" took place. Lana gave the house to her Mother. Before her feet could touch the paved driveway a huge mastiff bum rushed the opened car door. Lana's phone dropped in between her seat and console as the 200-pound dog launched its self-inside. Milli's hind legs were planted on the ground as she stood up leaning in the car as if she was hugging Lana and smiling with her tongue lolling around happily.

"Milli, Milli, my baby. You miss me, don't you? Lana said. "What mom-mom doing?" Lana said walking up and into the house.

"Mom!" Lana called out walking through the house. Nobody was in there. Milli barked.

"Where she at?" Lana asked. Milli lead her to the back door. Through the screen Lana could see her mother knelled down in her garden.

"Hey Mom! You look like grandma did in her garden," Lana called out as she neared her mother.

Her mom shielded the sun from her eyes as she looked up in Lana's direction. Lana could see her mother smiling as she neared. Since Lana had gotten out of the mental hospital, their relationship and bond had strengthened. They talked on the phone every day and went out to shop, go to the movies or to eat at least three times a week together.

"Hello Lanie," Lareen Watson said as Lana helped her up, they embraced and Lana kissed her mother's cheek in between the row of green tomatoes. "Lanie you taking care of yourself? Remember to take it easy and take your pills." Lareen gave Lana that all knowing look that only a mother gives their child.

"I am mom," Lana said walking arm in arm with her mom headed to the house. "I'm taking those crazy pills."

Lareen stopped at the back door. "Lanie they are not crazy pills. Its medication and perfectly normal."

Lana looked down sheepishly ashamed that she caused her mother any worry by her condition. She knew her mom stressed over her. Lana always wanted to take care of her mother and give her the world. Lana remembered vividly how hard it was for her mother raising her alone sometimes working two jobs. Lana vowed as a teenager to never disappoint her mother and to give her everything she deserves when she was able.

"Mom, I'm taking my meds every day when I'm supposed to. Matter of fact its time I take one now." Lana sat her MK pocketbook on the kitchen table and fished through it. Her mom washed her hands and poured a glass of sweet tea for Lana. Lana retrieved a small bottle uncapped it then shook one tiny white pill into her palm. She put the pill inside her mouth and accepted the glass from her mom. Her mother watched as Lana tilted her head back as she swallowed the tea.

"The doctors told me to relax so Isis is taking me to the Bahamas."

"That's good. Y'all girls go have fun and enjoy life."

Lana responded back in her best Caribbean accent, "Me just stopping by to grab a few things and say goodbye." They both laughed.

Lana went into her room and pulled out her aluminum magnesium Rimowa Topas suitcase. Before Lana threw a couple outfits bathing suits and feminine products into the bulky case she spit out the pill she had taken. Lana then took both of her hands and pressed on the outer rim of a mirror that was on a wall above a mahogany dresser. Her hands were position 10 and 2 around the mirror. Lana pressed hard huffing.

"Uughh!" Nothing happened. Lana inhaled then pushed hard grunting. "Uhggg!" The mirror popped open with a mechanical clink.

"Haven't been in you in a minute." Lana said.

The circumference of the mirror was 24 inches around. The hole in back of it was the same in diameter, it was approximately two feet deep.

"Oh, I was looking for you." Lana said placing a diamond-studded bangle around her wrist.

She threw two stacks of five thousand into the suitcase before zipping it up. Lana looked back into the open safe that still held a few rubber band stacks of cash and two 9mm pistols. She hadn't held a gun in almost a year. Lana grinned before placing the 9 inside her MK.

"Mom!" Lana called out. Her mother was still in the kitchen.

"Here take this sweet potato pie for you and Isis. Y'all girls have fun."

Lana hugged and kissed her mother. "We will, I love you mom. Talk to you when we land," Lana said as she pulled her suitcase out the house.

"Oh!" Lana's mother said as she hurried outside to Lana placing her luggage into her trunk, "here's a prescription of your meds, I went to the pharmacy a couple of days ago." Lana just looked at the white bag her mother held out to her for a second.

"Thanks," Lana said forcing a smile, "love you Mommy, see you soon." After getting into her car she looked around for Milli.

"Milli! Milli! "Lana yelled out, "Mom where she at?"

Lana's mom responded, "She is probably somewhere messing with that horse."

"Alright," Lana said, "call you when we land."

Gerald watched Kalana pull out of the yard from the side of the horse stalls. He grimaced in pain as he took his t-shirt off and wrapped it tightly around his bleeding forearm. He kneeled over Milli who lay in the golden dirt on her side, bleeding and breathing heavily. When the mastiff whined and whimpered Gerald grabbed the hilt of the bowie knife that he had plunged in Milli's neck, then twisted it silencing the dog permanently. Gerald was taking by surprised by Milli who didn't bark, she just attacked from out of nowhere. With Milli on the offense Gerald gave the vicious dog his forearm while he retrieved his knife strapped to his lower leg. The weight and momentum of the dog knocked Gerald on his back. Milli's powerful jaws were applying pressure by the second on Gerald's bicep when he disabled the dog. Gerald rubbed both sides of the big knife on Milli's thick black fur, cleaning it off before re-shifting it under his pants leg and headed toward the blue house.

Fifteen minutes into Lana's drive to the airport, she heard her phone going off under her seat. After a few failed attempts to reach it Lana finally grasped the phone to see it was Kush.

"Family!" Lana said when she answered the FaceTime call to see Kush.

"I've been tryna call you girl!" Kush stated. Through a haze of marijuana smoke Lana could see a couple gray strands in the dark-skinned Kush's beard.

"Where you at, we gotta hit the airport," Kush said. He smiled and his eyes brightened to the beautiful sight of Lana.

"You checking up on me now?" Lana said playfully, "I'm on my way to BWI now. You gonna sit with me on the plane too?"

Before Kush could respond another call was beeping in from a number under a name of G. Lana remembered to the fine guy that she met at the casino a couple days ago.

"Hold on for one second Kush, I have another call." Lana hit the answer button switching from the FaceTime call to a regular one.

"Hello Handsome," Lana spoke visualizing the man named G's pretty light brown eyes.

"Bitch! If you care ANYTHING about your dear mom, you'd get your ass back to her house pronto bitch!"

Lana heard the click ending the call but sat with the phone up to her ear baffled and stuck. The Audi screeched to a halt then bust a U turn nearly hitting a white F150. When Lana called Kush back via FaceTime, he could see before any words were spoken that something was wrong. Tears were streaming from wild eyes that were soft and joyful only seconds ago.

"Kush, I think someone has my mother!" Kush couldn't believe what Lana was telling him.

"What?" he asked frowning. Lana's words and sentences were running into one another.

"I'm going back to her house. Imma call her, I'll hit you back!"

Before Kush could get out, "Wait for me to get there..." Lana had ended the call. Kush looked at the time. It was 6:11, he was in Dover it would take him half hour to get to Greenwood to the ranch house. Kush let out a loud sigh as he made a U-ey, gunning the engine of the Land Cruiser heading south on US 13.

CHAPTER 10

Kish's Decision

Kish took a red eye at 3 o'clock in the morning headed for the Cayman Islands. She thought of her uncle Agent Rodgers, The Family and ultimately her badge. Just yesterday morning she had set Icy Bezel up with five kilos of pure cocaine, enough for a lifetime sentence to anyone with a prior criminal record such as Icy Bezel. Kish felt remorseful for what she had done to Icy Bezel. She was supposed to be the liaison to the Family and the Mexican informant. Instead in the heat of the moment, Kish made a split-second decision, acting with her heart. She received a call from the Office of Professional Responsibility, the FBI's equivalent of Internal Affairs, after finishing her report up on THE DIAMOND STATE MAFIA.

"Agent Moore?"

The unnaturally flat voice of the man who greeted himself as Special Agent Hagerty of the OPR, Kish felt was full of skepticism. He ordered her to report to the Philadelphia office immediately. The Ben Stein sounding man ended the call after Kish acknowledged that she would follow her last directive given by him. She instantly called Agent Rodgers, her superior and adopted Uncle.

At 3 a.m. it wasn't a surprise to Kish that he would be awake. He sounded down and his words slurred. Kish could tell he was up drinking.

"Tykish, you gave me no choice. I-I" It only took Kish two seconds to realize what her Uncle G was saying.

"YOU!" Kish hissed, "you threw me under the bus to the OPR!" Rodgers let out an aggravated sigh.

"Why did you Kill the Mexican informant?! I should have been pulled you! Are you a Federal Agent or a common thug?"

Kish raised her voice over Rodgers as she sobbed. "You have some fucking nerve. You should be asking yourself that!"

Agent Rodgers tone grew intense and boom through the phone, "You're fuckin' DONE! Just report in and hand over your credentials and firearm!"

Kish's sniffles were all that could be heard in the silence that followed Rodgers remarks. When he spoke again he was much calmer and his voice softer.

"If you comply by reporting in ASAP and handing over your creds, charges will not be filed. Let me repeat myself. Charges WILL NOT be filed on you, Kish!"

That was the last sentence Kish listened to from Agent Rodgers before she hung up on him. Kish drove to her real home in Bear, Delaware in silence with the radio turned off, deep into her thoughts. As soon as she turned the light on to her one storied brick home, the pictures in the living room caused a flood of memories.

Pictures of her father, grandparents and herself as she grew older peppered the armoire, stands and walls of the house. Up until the last photo that was taken of Kish, her induction ceremony into the FBI. Kish rationalized that she had no other choice for the acts she was about to commit. She walked into the walk-in closet in her bedroom. There under the hems of her dresses that hung up on the left side she pulled out two suitcases.

One of the suitcases held all the money she had made with the Family. Kish had accumulated a sum well over a hundred thousand. Kish always kept a suitcase ready for traveling, with a few outfits and a couple of bathing suits. Kish had jacked with X, Lana and Isis plus mastered the coke and heroin trade with Icy Bezel, O.G., and Kush. At this point, Kish didn't have one single ally she could confide in or turn to. With that in mind, she walked out of her house immediately with the two suitcases, with her mind made up. Kish headed to BWI, not to catch a flight to Philadelphia to the OPR but a one-way ticket to the Cayman Islands.

CHAPTER 11

Gerald's Revenge

When Kush's white Land Cruiser crept up the long driveway, he saw Lana's Audi parked haphazardly with the driver's door wide open. Kush stopped the SUV halfway up the lane. He put the gear in neutral, pressed both of the air condition buttons and then hit the start/stop engine button. The side of the black console opened up, revealing a Heckel and Koch P-30. Kush chambered a bullet as he kneeled on one knee, calculating the best way to approach the house.

Pinpointing his best route, Kush cautiously advanced forward taking cover behind two trees before reaching the rear of Lana's German machine. From the car Kush dashed to the side of the house. In a stooped walk, Kush rested his right hand firmly on top of the left one that held the P-30. Kush's right shoulder rubbed against the house as he circled the house crouched low. He listened intently under windows as he moved quietly around the house. Kush's cream-colored Route 13 shirt picked up a blue residue as he slid his shoulder against the paint. He felt thuds from the house vibrating through his shoulder before his ears heard anything.

One would think Kush's adrenaline was seeping steadily and slowly into his bloodstream. He had all the symptoms of a wicked adrenaline rush; increased heart rate, increased blood pressure, expanded air passages and enlarged pupils but his nerves were harnessed. His awareness and senses were acute. Kush had smelled death in the air as soon as he pulled up. The room was on the back-left corner of the home. It had two windows, one on each side. Kush got under the window that faced the sweeping back yard. The thuds that he had felt were now heavy thumps.

He heard the voices of two people in the room. One was weak and pleading, the other violent and hateful. The small, feeble voice wept and moaned, in pain and sorrow. Even with the persons mouth gagged Kush understood her cries.

"Get off her! STOP IT!!" The monstrous sounding male's voice repeated questions tauntingly.

"You watching? You see this?"

Standing up, Kush stood to the side of the window trying to get a glimpse inside the room. A tiny sliver at the bottom of the closed flora-patterned, beige curtain was the only view inside. The small slit only obscured his view. He could see a body part that he couldn't identify, moving in a repetitive motion. The thumping was in sync with the movement Kush was seeing. Kush's mind registered fast what was taking place. He moved further down the back of the house headed to the backdoor when the thumping and knocking grew more rapidly and intense. Kush crept up to the back door, which was open but the storm door was closed. He peered inside the kitchen through the storm door's glass. Not knowing how many hostile people were in the house, Kush raised his pistol as he quietly opened the storm door. With sure steps, Kush moved through the kitchen. He swung his body swiftly into the first room's corner, which was the living room with his gun aimed. Pastel pink and yellow colors decorated the empty living room. Kush heard the males voice loud and clear now that he was in the house. The sinister and cold voice resonated through the house. Each word was filled with emotion and lingered like a cloud of heavy smoke in the still air.

"Did you see THAT 'ol lady?" As Kush stepped down the hallway quietly to the bedroom he listened to the mans' revengeful tirade.

Gerald's muscles bulged and glistened as he stood in between the two defenseless women. His normal short curly hair now laid down flat from perspiration. Sweat rolled off of his heaving chest and dropped to Lana's bare backside. She was bent over her mother's bed, with her arms stretched out over her head and hands cuffed. Gerald's eyes were full of rage as he looked down to the unresponsive Lana. Gerald knew he had plowed through Lana's vagina like a train but she didn't make a sound the whole time. Not even a tear or grimace from pain. This only enraged Gerald more. He wanted to hurt Lana's soul before he tortured her to death.

Lana gave herself to Gerald peacefully and willingly by the leverage Gerald held in his hands when she arrived to the house. She jumped out of her car to the horrifying sight of a man with a gun up to her mother's head. Mrs. Watson's head rested in the crook of Gerald's big left arm as he stood behind her. He held a 45 automatic in the right hand with it pressed firmly to heom's temple. Gerald handled Mrs. Watson roughly as they stood in the doorway of the blue house. Gray duck taped, pended her arms to her sides, it was crudely wrapped from her elbows down to her hands. Gerald threw a pair of handcuffs down to the ground.

"Put them cuffs on or I'll blow your moms brains out like you did my moms and little bro!" Lana followed every command Gerald gave praying that her submission would save her mother.

Mrs. Watson was partially dragged and choked as Gerald backpedaled through the house, leading the handcuffed Lana into the back room. There, he tore Lana's clothes off and raped her. She didn't resist. Gerald invaded her from the back all the while he kept his pistol trained on the seated Mrs. Watson. He made her mom watch him perform the cruel act. Frustrated from not getting the reaction from Lana that he wanted, Gerald's blood boiled. He snatched Lana's head back by grabbing a fist full of her hair. He twisted her head so that she faced her mother then pointed his pistol at Lana's mother. Lana starred into her mother's eyes as her mom said, "I love you," through the duct tape gag. Foam sat in the corners of his mouth as he yanked Lana's hair harder, pulling her closer while bending near her ear.

"This is revenge BITCH!"

"Boom!" Gerald squeezed the trigger causing the deafening sound. Lana's facial expression didn't flinch or twitch.

"Goodbye Bitch!" Gerald said now pressing the hot-barreled gun to Lana's cheek.

"Naw, bitch. You gonna beg!" Gerald said then commenced to pistol-whip Lana.

Kush kicked open the bedrooms door after Gerald had delivered over a half dozen blows to the still silent Lana. Gerald only had enough time to look into his killer's eyes for a split second before Kush placed a bullet in his forehead. "Boom!"

Gerald fell over the prone body of Lana, instantly dead. Kush rolled the dead weight of Gerald off of Lana to find that she was unconscious from the pistol whipping. Kush's face frowned and he shook his head at the condition he found Lana in. Lacerations on her head and face lay open painting the white and sky-blue patterned blanket dark red.

CHAPTER 12

X Cast Off

As soon as the Family's meeting was over at Aunt Mary's Soul Food, X called the Brooklyn native Coco on his way to the Seaford Marina. Coco greets X like a true 5 Percenter.

"Peace God, what's the knowledge?"

X didn't hesitate to dangle his golden carrot before Coco's eyes, which came in the form of money. He was willing to give up half of the million dollars that was on the Clara Lee.

"Yo, homie if you wanna make some big, big, big money meet me at the Seaford Marina in an hour. I'll be on the yacht named the Clara Lee!"

X hung up the phone confident that Coco would be there. He definitely needed another man with him. If for nothing else, just in helping pilot the Clara Lee. But X had a feeling that things were going to get messy in the Dominican Republic. He knew he needed an extra man but didn't want to include anyone in his Family. X couldn't stand to lose another family member, whether it be from getting killed, going to jail or losing their sanity. Lana's mental condition weighed heavily on X's heart. He rode in silence going south bound on 1-13. It wasn't a hard decision for X to choose Coco, a complete stranger to accompany him on this dangerous yet personal extraction. Coco met all of the criteria. He was young, ambitious and hungry. It takes a person that's not afraid of the unknown to go "OT" and not only thrive but also prosper. Coco's main man "Hos," short for "Hostile" had a cousin enrolled and staying on the campus of University of Delaware.

Coco and Hos arrived in Delaware from New York during the cousin's first semester. They had come down from the Big City with one ounce of crack between the both of them and by the forth semester they shared a whole kilo. X's last reason for picking Coco was because he was Hispanic. He could interpret for him and blend in perfectly.

When Coco boarded the Clara Lee forty-five minutes later, X was checking the vessel's fuel, coolant and oil levels. Coco looked around hesitant not sure of what to expect.

"Come on, Coco," X said, "you know I ain't tryna harm you or I would of let my cuz kill you when she slit your girls throat." Coco uncocked and tucked his Smith and Wesson pistol. "Follow me."

X lead Coco down below the deck to the main cabin. On the queen-sized bed lay two brief cases wide open. Inside the cases were neatly packed bills. Coco's eyes were glued to the currency and his thoughts went in a million and one directions.

"Half of that's all yours…if you come with me and help me." Coco took a step closer to the opened cases.

"How much is that?" Coco asked.

X responded, "That's what a million dollars looks like my G."

"Go with you where and do what?" Coco asked next, his eyes never leaving the money.

X sat on the bed and lit a blunt that he had had behind his ear. "To the Dominican Republic to get my family."

Coco took another step closer to the bed and briefcases. Slowly his hand stretched out to touch it to make sure this wasn't a dream. X slammed both cases down fast and hard. The sound echoed in the quite cabin causing Coco's eyes to divert from the closed cases to X.

Coco smiled. "How many niggas I gotta kill, cause it gotta be some wicked shit?!"

X stood and passed Coco the leaf rolled marijuana blunt. "Could be one or plenty, I don't know. But I need you and as you can see..." X gestured to the money. "This is very important to me."

Coco extended his hand immediately. "My name is Cory."

X shook his hand, "Yusuf."

MZ Rae exited the beautiful fortress of a bank. Palm trees lined both sides of the walkway leading to a taxicab cluttered round about. MZ Rae was tall and slim with natural, sandy brown hair that stopped just inches above her shoulders. Not only was she dressed professionally, but also very sophisticated. She was wearing a curvy Sharkskin Pencil skirt with a matching suit jacket, over a plum colored thin blouse. Black red bottom two-inch heels complimented her long slender brown legs. She radiated with business savvy and confidence. MZ Rae didn't think for one second that the bank was stalling her out, even if this was her fourth day on the island and her second to the bank.

The well-mannered bank assistant manager politely told her that tomorrow the withdrawal would be ready and complete. As far as she knew, the Family's agenda and plans hadn't been compromised. All she knew was the legality of the numbers and what she was doing was totally legal regarding the International Bank Laws. This was a corporation of business' cashing out on their shares and stocks. Her same cabbie that she had been using since she got off the plane, pulled up. Terence a dreadlocked cabbie from St. Martin jumped out and hurried to the other side of the cab to open the door for her.

"Where to now, Boss lady?" he said in broken English as he hopped back under the wheel.

"Take me to see more of your beautiful island," MZ Rae said.

"My pleasure to take you," Terrence said smiling.

He pulled off and adjusted the volume of his stereo so that Peter Tosh was heard behind the engine of the old cab.

MZ Rae felt giddy like she was a little girl again and why shouldn't she be. A half a million of that money was hers and she planned to open a full-service accounting firm. MZ Rae, whose real name was Lisa Rae, kicked her pumps off and stretched back. Her tension uncoiled like the slow unraveling of a fat snake. Instantly, the Caribbean scenery and Tosh's voice relaxed her; she felt safe with Terrence from the first ride with him at from the airport. He looked and sounded like all the Rastas she had seen in the movies. The cab was a derelict robust cab similar to the one Mr. T drove on the movie DC Cab. A brown pouch and two medallions dangled from his rearview mirror. One of the medallions had the face of Marcus Garvey and the other Malcolm X. She was amused as they talked. While he drove she found out that Terrence not only knew of Delaware but was familiar with the states corporation laws, the Firefly Music Festival and the Punkin Chunkin competitions that were once held outside of Bridgeville, near Coverdale Crossroads. Due to it being Pirate Week in the Cayman Islands, Terrence didn't have to take MZ Rae too far from her hotel to see beauty, astonishments and the colorful Island people celebrate their swashbuckling history and culture.

When MZ Rae made it back to her hotel it was after 10 p.m. The parades were over but people still filled the streets partying in full pirate attire. Terrence carried MZ Rae's bags of souvenirs, jewelry and clothes that she had bought, to her door. MZ Rae handed Terrence four crisp one hundred-dollar bills. He handed her two of them back.

"I was only on the clock half of the time."

MZ Rae smiled before saying, "Tomorrow nine o'clock sharp."

Terrence bowed his head. "Rodger that Boss lady."

The tall, dreadlocked Rasta did a little dance with a one-two step back and forth before walking off. To him MZ Rae was an angel in disguise. Before she had hopped into his cab he was two months behind in his rent and facing eviction at any day.

"All Praises to JAH the Most High!" Terrence yelled as he put the cab into reverse.

It didn't register to MZ Rae until she was in the bathroom naked about to jump into the shower, that music was playing. Wrapping herself in a towel, she hurried through the four-star suite. When she realized where the music was coming from, she stopped in her tracks. Gingerly and slowly MZ Rae stepped toward the opened sliding balcony doors. Aaliyah's voice sang seductively from her tenth-floor balcony.

"Who's there?" MZ Rae called out, but no one answered.

She stopped just before crossing the open portal to the outside balcony. MZ Rae stuck her head out first. To her surprise, Kish laid reclined back on a beach chair. Kish's skin glistened from perspiration in the Caribbean night heat. She wore a yellow two-piece bathing suit that complimented her dark skin.

"Hello Rae!" Kish said opening her eyes, sounding happy to see MZ

Rae.

"How'd you get in here?" was MZ Rae's response.

By MZ Rae not questioning what she was doing alive, Kish knew she hadn't talk to Lana in the last two days.

"I have my ways," Kish said with a devilish grin.

MZ Rae felt awkward. She pulled the towel up over her C cup size breast. Kish closed the four-foot gap between them fast.

"Don't you touch me!" MZ Rae said through clenched teeth while she backpedaled, until the teak wood-framed, queen-sized bed stopped her.

Kish stopped just inches short of MZ Rae. She put on a seductive face of curiosity as she licked her lips. Neither the grin nor the blatant lust in her eyes diminished, as she reached for MZ Rae.

"So you telling me I didn't make you feel good?" MZ Rae looked down at her polished toes as her towel fell around them.

Kush called the first person that came to his mind. The only person to ever patch him up and tend to his wounds back in his early corner days when he made a name for himself in the underworld.

"Sista Vic, Lana's been beat bad. She's fucked up!" Sista Vic was at her house in Seaford, Delaware packing for the flight to the Caymans. She stopped in her tracks.

"Damn it!" Sista Vic shouted, "what's her condition?"

Kush stuttered, unable to get his words out as he looked down at the beautiful girl.

Sista Vic questioned. "What's the girl doing, Kush?"

Kush moved the bloody hair from Lana's face. "She's unconscious.

And her head's bleeding bad, Sis!"

Sista Vic cut his words off abruptly, "Apply pressure to her wounds to try to stop the bleeding. Where are y'all at?"

Even with the flip phone up to his ear, Kush didn't hear Sista Vic's question.

"X gonna kill me. I'm supposed to be protecting you Queen B," Kush said solemnly out loud. Talking to Lana lying comatose on the bed.

Kush pulled Lana's sleeveless blouse down over her breast and pulled up jeans.

Sista Vic's high-pitched voice yelled, "KUSH, WHERE FUCK ARE YALL AT?!"

Kush responded, "Um Um…at the Greenwood ranch!"

In an unwavering and still voice Sista Vic spoke in a lower tone. Remaining calm because panicking causes bad decisions to be made.

"Kush stop her bleeding and talk to her. I'll be there in 15 minutes. Kush, she gonna be alright baby."

Kush took his shirt off and wrapped it tightly around Lana's head. He stood up when he was done and looked around the bedroom. Lana's mother was dead.

"Come on baby," he said to Lana as he scooped her up in his arms, "let's get out of here."

Kush took her down the hall to her own bedroom. He steady talked to her as he laid her on the bed and ran into the adjoining bathroom to wet a towel. Kush softly dabbed and stroked Lana's face with the cold towel. Kush got on his knees beside the bed close to Lana's right ear as he wiped blood from her eyes. He never stopped talking to Lana who snored lightly like she just sleeping and mumbled occasionally. Kush felt himself being pulled into Lana's beautiful unblemished face.

"Come on Lanie. Ain't that what X call you?" Kush said, "you pretty as hell girl. Um, Lanie you know I always had a thing for you but X my Brother and…"

"And what?" Lana said with closed eyes.

CHAPTER 13

O.G. & ISIS

O.G. and Isis drove straight from Aunt Mary's Soul Food restaurant to BWI airport in Baltimore MD. When Isis had finally given in to O.G.'s unrelenting sexual advances, she was upset with herself that she hadn't sooner. It was after The Family had killed the Le Eme Cartel member. Isis and O.G. took the duty of getting rid of the Cholo's body while Kish and Icy Bezel took the bricks of cocaine to a safe house. It was Isis' idea to feed the dead Mexican to the chickens.

"So, what we gonna do with him?" O.G. asked looking down at the naked corpse frozen into an awkward position.

"It's an axe back there." Isis said pointing to the back yard.

She watched O.G. remove the sleek but stiff and uncomfortable bulletproof vest. His sweat drenched t-shirt clung to his thick muscular upper body.

"Chop 'em up and let the chickens feed on 'em," Isis said with a little giggle.

She diverted her eyes away from O.G. as he looked up, not wanting him to see that she was checking him out.

He turned his lips up like, "Yea right!"

"WE!" O.G. said before bending down to pick the corpse up. He threw the dead weight over his shoulder like a sack of potatoes before finishing his sentence. "Can chop 'em up together."

O.G. headed for the back door of the house; he thought, *"She didn't even flinch when I said that she would have to chop him!"*

He was aroused by her poise and at the same time Isis' sassiness.

O.G.'s penis swelled slightly and a vision of him standing with Isis's legs in the bend of his arms as she rode his manhood slowly, popped into mind. O.G. stopped outside in the backyard at a big slab of wood from an oak tree.

"Get that," he told Isis pointing to the axe stuck in the center of the four feet wide chopping block.

Isis struggled to pull the axe free from its resting place. Once she had moved it, O.G. positioned the body on its knees with the head placed on the wood. O.G. had seen and done with his own two hands some gruesome shit, which all still haunt him on some nights, but he'd never witnessed a woman do a gory act like dismembering a body. O.G. was intrigued, amused and turned on all at the same time.

The late nights summer air held a thick fog, almost a mist. The Delaware humidity had Isis' skin sweaty. She felt as though she looked swarthy. So being attractive was the very last thought on her mind. But through all the night's happenings, at this very moment O.G.'s mind and every thought was on Isis. With her hair out of place and her clothes sweated through, O.G.'s erection grew harder as the moonlight made the top of her small cleavage shine. He licked then bit down on his bottom lip as Isis hiked up her skirt and widen her stance in preparation to take a swing of the axe. Isis small but curvy and toned frame wavered then shook as she pulled the axe up high over her head. Her eyes narrowed, trained on the back of the dead man's neck. She let out a loud grunt like Serena Williams as she came down with all her might.

"AHHHHGG!" Isis mighty swing was halted on its decline before connecting with its target.

O.G. had caught the axe's wooden handle just below the wedge. He snatched the axe from Isis. Letting the axe drop to the ground, O.G. pulled Isis close to him. Isis didn't resist the aggressive but not so rough kiss. She felt through O.G.'s lip lock, his deep yearning, strength and gentleness. The rush that stirred within her was similar to the burst of adrenaline she had an hour before, when the bullets were flying. Isis returned O.G.'s kiss with the same intensity and passion. While giving and receiving tongue and nibbling on O.G.'s lip, Isis pushed the dead Cholo off the chunk of wood with her foot. She pulled O.G. by his wet t-shirt towards her, as she backpedaled two steps until the back of her calves touched the chunk of wood. Isis lay down on the slab of oak and opened her legs, panty less. O.G. broke his belt as he tore off his pants.

"HMMM!" Isis said out loud on the plane. Her body temperature spiked as she relived that long and fulfilling night.

She looked over to her left to O.G. who bobbed his head listening to Pimp C through headphones. He returned her look after feeling her eyes on him. Isis reached over between O.G.'s legs and cuffed his crotch. O.G. looked around to see if anyone on the sparsely occupied flight were awake or paying attention them. The lights were dim on the late-night flight, with only a few passengers' personal lamps on. They shared a mischievous smile before giving in to their desires. Isis straddled O.G. She pulled the soft blanket that the stewardess had given her, around her back and over both of their heads.

Thirty minutes later after the both of them were spent, O.G. fell asleep instantly. Isis noticed that someone had been texting her phone. She had never seen the phone number before. The text messages read: *Ice, you'll be forever my sister and nothing can break the bond we have. No, I'm not dead and no, I'm not a FED! But I do want that money! Sis, me and you. This is our chance! A two-way split! Do the math bitch that's THREE FUCKIN MILLION apiece. Let's get rich, Bitch!*

Isis first impulse was to wake up O.G. to show him the text. But during the eight seconds it took her to shake him awake, she had come to the conclusion that she should rethink this two-way split proposition.

"What up babe?" O.G. asked yawning.

"Nothing," Isis said, "go back to sleep baby." Isis rubbed his chest slow in a circular motion. She stared out of the planes window into the purplish black sky. "Sky's the limit. Right?"

Hours later after landing at Owen Roberts Airport, O.G. and Isis went to a restaurant to eat some traditional island food. They then checked into a hotel, one block away from Beasley Bros. International bank. O.G. asked Isis a few times was she alright.

"You're not acting like yourself," he said.

Isis' thoughts were on the proposition that Kish had made her. Later that night, in the a.m., Isis and O.G. made patient and passionate love. Afterwards Isis stood buck-naked over a snoring O.G. She held a knife high in the air. She had stolen it from the restaurant they had eaten at earlier. Tears started to well up in her eyes just before she drove the knife down into her sleeping lover. The blade entered into O.G.'s temple up to the knife's hilt. O.G.'s body seized up and his eyes fluttered then opened. Killing him instantly. Isis felt his lifeless eyes staring through her soul. She closed O.G.'s eyes then took a deep breath, fighting to hold herself together.

"Tomorrow it'll be worth it," Isis justified to herself.

"And what?" Lana repeated herself now opening her eyes.

Kush sat speechless looking down into Lana's eyes. He was relieved seconds later when Sista Vic pulled up. Kush rushed out of the room and house to meet Sista Vic. Anything to avoid the topic he and Lana were on. Kush carried Sista Vic's black bag when he lead her into Lana's room.

"AWW Baby girl," Sista Vic said sounding motherly as she hugged and kissed Lana, "so sorry about your mother."

Lana said nothing. Her eyes told Sista Vic everything as silent tears ran down her face. Sista Vic waved Kush out the room. She continues talking to Lana when he was gone.

"Baby, ain't no time to give up on life. This is not your fault! Your mama was proud of you and KNEW you loved her dearly!" Sista Vic helped Lana up to a sitting position as she continued to talk to her. She unwrapped the blood-stained shirt from Lana's head.

"Imma fix you up, baby and we gotta go, Lanie. We gotta go."

Sista Vic gave Lana two 30-milligram Percocet pills, before she started stitching up the gash on the side of Lana's head. As the needle went in and out of her flesh Lana didn't grimace or show any signs of pain that the procedure felt painful. She just stared blankly. After she was finished with that wound, Sista Vic moved to the opening high on Lana's forehead, near the hairline. When Sista Vic was finished she cleaned around the stitching and placed a slim bandage that blended in perfectly with Lana's complexion. Sista Vic smoothed the bandage one time over with her two index fingers. She shook her head pitifully as she looked down at Lana, who still sat silent and unresponsive. Sista Vic gently grabbed Lana's chin and guided her face up until their eyes met.

"Queen B, Kalana. Lanie, you're gonna have to say goodbye to your mother." For the first time since the altercation Lana showed emotion. Her cries became audible as she hugged Sista Vic tightly.

"Go in there and pay your last respects to her physical form, because best believe her spirit and essence won't leave your side!"

Two hours later, approximately at 2:45 a.m., the trio of Kush, Sista Vic and Lana boarded a plane out of D.C.'s Dulles International. They held their breath as they went through Customs, not knowing if they were already wanted women and man by state and/or federal authorities. Once on the plane they all shared a huge sigh of relief. With the help of two more Percocet, Lana fell into a coma-like sleep. She dreamt of her mother and father reuniting on the other side.

Agent Rodgers tossed and turned in his empty king-sized bed. He was restless. The plan to bring down the Diamond State Mafia played over and over in his mind. The Cayman Island authorities would apprehend MZ Rae, when she exits the bank. The manager of the bank informed Agent Rodgers yesterday that that would be the last day they the bank could legally hold The Families millions. Once MZ Rae was in the custody of the Cayman Island Police, federal warrants would be issued for the all of the Diamond State Mafia members that were stateside.

He figured a shot of scotch would help him sleep. He got out of his bed and went into his kitchen where he pulled out a fifth of Johnnie Walker Black Label out the cupboard. On his second shot, his cell phone rang. It wasn't rare for Agent Rodgers to receive early morning calls from superiors or his subordinates. But for some reason he know that this call had bad vibes written all over it.

"Hello!" It was Agent Russell his next in command.

"Boss, she's gone! Agent Moore caught a flight out to the Caymans!" Agent Rodgers tried to speak before swallowing the strong liquor in its entirety and ended up choking, then spiting it out of his mouth.

"What?!" he yelled when he caught his breath, "check all those mothafuckas in that Family that we have under investigation, for flights out of the country!"

Rodgers hung up the phone then took a long gulp of scotch from the bottle. Five minutes later his phone rang again. Rodgers answered on the first ring.

"What?" Rodgers said angrily. There was a long pause before Agent Russell spoke.

"They're gone. All of them accept Yusef Watson took flights to the Cayman Islands. But...even he hasn't been sighted by any of our people in over twelve hours."

Agent Rodgers replied, "Fuck Me!" Before hanging up the phone.

Agent Rodgers looked at the time on his phone screen, it read 3:45 a.m. He hesitated to call his superior. Then said, "Fuck it!"

Picking up his phone he scrolled down his contact list stopping a DEPUTY. Short for Deputy Director. He took another long pull off the fifth bottle while he waited for his call to be answered. Agent Rodgers hung up then called back after the DP's voicemail picked up. On the first ring the phone was answered this time.

"George, this better be good!" a groggy voice stated.

Agent Rodger words stuttered when he talked fast.

"Ye-Ye-Yes Si- Sir," he finally stammered out, "all of the members on the Diamond State case have fled to the Cayman Islands."

Agent Rodgers wouldn't dare take a breath and give the DP room to interrupt him, "We previously were going to place warrants on all of them tomorrow once their accountant walked out of the bank with the money."

The DP interrupted the babbling Agent, "What do you want? It's three in the morning for Christ sake!"

Rodgers spoke immediately, "I need you to confirm an international extraction for me and my men."

"Hold the fuck up!" the DP spat, "the answer is NO! You had your chance Rodgers."

Rodgers tried to further explain but the DP talked over him.

"Put an international warrant on each and every member that went abroad. Unless they step foot on U.S. soil your duty is over on this case. Move on!" Were his boss' last words before hanging up.

"FUCK!" Agent Rodgers screamed as he threw the fifth bottle across his kitchen, "you Muthafuckas think you can outsmart me!" His voice echoed through his big empty house, "Imma get every last one of you Black Bastards!"

CHAPTER 14

New Friends

With hearing a males voice calling out from above deck, X and Coco released their handshake. Both men grabbed their guns and pointed it at the other.

"Who the fuck is that?" X asked through clenched teeth with his Colt 45 revolver trained on Coco.

Coco's semi-automatic 9mm was only inches away from touching the barrow of X's revolver. He held the pistol steadily, aiming back at X.

"Them niggas ain't with me!" was Coco's response as he bit down on his lip, "Word on everything, I came by myself!"

X lowered his roscoe first. Turned and ran to the bed grabbing the two suitcases, he concealed them behind the yacht's bar that held at least ten different colorful fifth bottles of various spirits. More voices could be heard now and they were getting closer. Coco followed X's lead by tucking his pistol in the small of his back. X then motioned for him to come over to the bar as he started to pour two shots from a fifth of Tanqueray. The two men toasted as the voices from the unknown and unwelcomed men grew even closer to them.

Coco narrowed his eyes and pointed his finger to X. "You gonna make me rich?!" Coco said. His endorphins had shot their load when he had seen all that money. *"It's my time!"* Coco's inner voice screamed out.

He knew that this was that moment in life where one came upon the proverbial fork in the road. The image of those blue faced Ben Franklins lined up in those cases, haunted him since he had laid eyes on it. This was way different than him hustling and dreaming in the streets saying, "I'm grinding to see a million." He couldn't believe that he had actually just seen a million dollars and it was right here in his grasp. Everything was happening so fast but Coco already determined that he would ride this huge wave to the end to get that money.

X shook his head slow but confident and true. "Imma make you rich."

Three men appeared a split second later. Both X and Coco came to the conclusion that they were Italians.

"We almost got lost on this humongous boat!" The smaller one of the three men at 6' 1,'' said chuckling.

"Yes, the Clara Lee is a beauty," X said smiling to Coco who shook his head in agreement.

The two bigger Italian stood on each side of the man speaking. They both carried pistols, the taped handles pressed up against their pasta filled stomachs. The statement of their blatantly displayed untraceable pistols wasn't overlooked by X or Coco.

"My name is Geegee," the dark-skinned Sicilian that appeared to be in his early thirties said as he walked over to the bar and motioned X to pour him a shot of the strong gin. The room was dead silent while Geegee threw back the shot.

"This is…or well was my father's boat," he said looking at X, "what the fuck are you doing on it?"

X smiled as he poured him and Coco another shot. "You know how I got it. I did you a solid in killing the people who killed your father." X and Coco toasted again and downed the shot in one gulp.

"I got the key off a dead pig and fine ass Japanese chick that murdered your father!" The middle-aged Sicilian shook his head in agreement.

"Paulie. Vinnie. You guys wanna shot of this shit?" Geegee asked the two men that came in with him. They both declined silently. As Geegee poured himself another shot he talked, "I know you killed that dirty fuckin' pig and that Jap bitch. Much appreciation."

Geegee reached over the bar, extending his hand. X looked at Coco then down at Geegee's hairy hand. X barley lifted his hand up and within a blink of his eyes he felt Geegee's firm handshake. Geegee's black eyes stared directly at X and his grip grew firmer by the second. X's eyes never fell from the Italian's, as he matched the man's strong handshake and stare down.

"And I also KNOW what my Father left behind on this yacht!" X pulled back his hand from Geegee's grip and drew the pistol.

Coco followed X's actions by doing the same. The two Italians that flanked Geegee's sides, X just knew they would drawl their heat back on him and Coco. X figured him and Coco could kill them and be off going south down the Pacific in ten minutes. The two capos, along with Geegee, just looked back at X and Coco. Not looking threatened nor were they threatening. Their body language showed no aggression.

"Put those things away," Geegee said with a slight wave of his hand. X and Coco complied. As Geegee continued to talk he filled Coco's, X's and his shot glasses.

"The boat is a gift for my father but before you lay claim to that shit load of money," Geegee positioned X and Coco's filled to the brim shot glasses in front of them. "You have to do another job for me." Geegee handed each man his drink, then picked up his own. "Just one hit and all of that is yours!" He raised his glass.

"Hold up, Pizon," Coco said, "but I don't know this nigga or know nothing about what's going on." X grabbed Coco's bicep as the New Yorker attempted to take a step towards the Italians. "Imma go head and excuse myself," Coco stated to Geegee.

"What you doing, dog?" X asked Coco. "Give us a second," X said to Geegee then pulled Coco back, about five feet away.

"Look," Coco started, "this some other shit then what you explained to me. I thought we were going to DR. I don't fuck with these Alfredo eating mutherfuckers."

X cut him off… "I got a million for you. That's how much that is," X said directing his eyes down to the suitcases, "do this with me and help me get my family and it's all yours. I got more coming."

Coco saw nothing but truth in X's eyes. He agreed with one single nod. They stepped back up to the bar and raised their drinks to Geegee.

CHAPTER 15

Alive

Evita's eyes popped open at the first sound of gunfire.

"Plaaatack!"

The digital clock on her nightstand read 4:44 a.m. Within seconds all of her thoughts and concern were on her daughter's safety.

"Where are you Hector?" Evita said out loud seeing he wasn't in bed.

Evita threw off the cover and hit the floor. She army crawled a few feet until she was close to her nightstand. Reaching up Evita opened the drawer to her nightstand. Her small hand sought franticly inside the drawer before it touched the cold piece of steel. Evita retrieved a Taurus 85 ultra-lite .38 special with the mother of pearl handle. She stayed low and close to the walls, as she made her way down the hall to her daughters room. A three-shot spurt could be heard from the front of the house as Evita pushed open Ximena's bedroom door. The baby was still sound asleep in her bed. Evita picked the toddler up and headed back to her room. Evita ran swiftly down the hall. Shouts and voices became louder echoing off the walls and high ceiling of the house.

She knew they were inside. Evita ran through her bedroom into a black and white huge shower/bathroom. The room's walls alternated, black, white, black, white. The ceiling was black and floor white. A gigantic black tub sat on the white onyx floor at the forefront of the shower. Evita hunkered down in back of the black tub. She hugged her baby tight, resting her back against the cold stone. Evita laid Mena down softly on the cold floor when she heard voices inside her bedroom. She cocked the hammer back on the .38 revolver. Evita's black cabernet satin pajamas clung to her sweaty plump and curvy physique. She moved around to the front of the tub.

Distancing herself from her daughter. Driven strictly by instinctually impulse, like the lioness protected her cub. Aiming the pistol at the arched door less room entrance. Evita's hand trembled as the approaching steps and voices became even louder.

"POW!" Evita let off one shot at the first glimpse of a person.

"Evy!" Hector yelled out, "Evy, you shot me!" Hector's ear was bleeding.

Evita's shot had grazed his left ear taking a small piece off. "Evita! Everything's alright!"

Evita lowered the smoking gun and fell into Hector's embrace. "What the fuck is going on?" Evita questioned.

"Dadda. Dadda!"

They both looked down to see Mena with outstretched arms. Hector picked the baby up. Evita tried to grab the baby from Hector's arms.

"Your dripping blood from your ear."

Evita!" a voice called out from inside their adjoined bedroom.

She froze at hearing a voice she knew well. Evita gave up on her efforts to take Ximena from Hector as she moved forward raising the pistol. There in her bedroom stood Fame, one half of the soulless twin assassins.

"You dirty mutha!" Evita screamed aiming her gun at Fame.

Hector grabbed her from behind and snatched the 38 out of her hands. Evita sprinted over to Fame leaning on her long-mirrored vanity. He was head to toe in black Dickies. He held a Mach 11 with the impact brace and extended clip.

Fame didn't react to the blows and haymakers that Evita unleashed on him.

"You fucking killed him…You killed X!...You killed him!" A chubby older man in a black fedora with a face of pain tucked his Colt 45 in his waist then peeled Evita off of Fame.

"Evita, sit down." Fame said calmly in Spanish. She still kicked and screamed threats, trying in vain to escape the man's hold. "Sit the fuck down!" Fame said now raising his voice along with the Mach 11. He pointed at Hector holding Ximena. Evita stopped resisting and slowly sat on her bed.

"Uncle, take brotha Hector and the little princess into the living room." Evita looked at Hector in disbelief. She knew he wasn't a fighter or from the streets but she thought he had a little spine. Hector didn't protest as the chubby man took Evita's pistol from his hand and ushered him and Ximena out of the room. Closing the door behind them, fame let the sub machinegun hang by its strap from his shoulder while he took off one of his black gloves to light a Capone cigar. Evita sat on the edge of the bed with her head down in her hands, crying. Fame took a few pulls from the strong tobacco before speaking.

"I'm just here for your treacherous brother, El OSO and your soft ass fiancé," Fame laughed, "but I'm not gonna kill him." He made a mock gun with his hand and curled his finger like he was pulling a trigger. "But El OSO gon die."

"Fuck him!" Evita screamed, "you killed mi muthafuckin baby X for him! So fuck you and him!" Fame busted out laughing.

He was thinking of what the before/after picture would look like when he gives Evita the news that X is living. She looked at Fame with disgust before resuming her previous position of her elbows on her knees and head buried in hands.

Fame limped over to Evita. The shots from Det. Way and Angie Wu had crippled Fame. He had no feeling in his left leg. It felt numb and cold to him like a piece of him were dead. Fame sat on the bed beside Evita.

"I hate you, Fuma! Diablo!" Evita said coldly.

"If you be quiet for one minute, you'll have a change of heart," Fame interjected.

Evita gave one last, "Fuck You!" before shutting up.

"El OSO was behind Jesus' murder…" Evita shut her eyes tight, but that didn't stop the tears from spilling. That thought has crossed her mind more than a few times since her "good brother's" death.

"Me and Hector's partnering up," Fame said with a smile, "once El OSO is toppled, I'll be king. This is for Jesus and Peppe." Fame made the sign of the cross and kissed it to the sky.

Evita nodded her head slowly in agreement tears streaking her cheeks.

"See," Fame said, "I told you you'll have a change of heart about me." Evita's smile evaporated.

"One more thing," Fame said standing up with a little difficulty. Evita waved Fame away, "X is alive."

Fame said as he turned and walked toward the bedroom's door. He stopped and faced Evita again after he opened the door.

"Huh!" Fame said under his breath cracking a smile.

Had to find humor in the twist of fates. A whole five seconds passed before Fame's words registered to Evita.

"What you say?" she asked Fame who stood at the opened door.

Fame shook his head. "You heard me," he said now grinning.

His smiled displaying two twinkling gold teeth as he nodding his head, "Your homeboy is still living."

Evita frowned. "Are you for real?" Fame blew smoke out from the cigar as he sighed heavily.

"Yeah, I'm fucking serious. I just talk to him a couple days ago." Evita jumped up and squeezed Fame almost knocking him over.

"I love you Fame, I love you!" She kissed Fame all over his face.

Fame pushed her off of him. "You're welcome," he said.

Evita beamed, her eyes, smile, and body language screamed total elation.

"He's been alive this WHOLE time," she said as she paced back and forth.

"It's a long story, but he was locked up and he just came home." Fame smiled again. "Probably on his way down here."

Evita just stared out into space looking at her reflection from her dresser's mirror. Thinking of X seeing his daughter for the first time made tears of joy streamed down her cheeks.

"Hey!" Fame said snapping Evita out of her trance. "Get your baby, all the cash you can take from Hector and bounce!"

CHAPTER 16

Caymen Island

Former Special Agent Rodgers watched the impressive Beasley Bros. International bank from across the street. The Cayman Island Constable joined him. The constable had two plain-clothes officers on each end of the street. Rodgers scowled when he seen Kish in the back of the yellow cab with MZ Rae. Even though Rodgers had totally disregarded his superior's direct order and was clearly out of his jurisdiction he still convinced himself that he was delivering justice. The constables cell phone rang. The popular anthem to the TV show Cops sang out.

"Aye. This is he," the constable replied to the caller.

The middle-aged, bald-headed stout Caribbean stroked his salt and peppered goatee. Slowly he looked over to Rodgers who sat in the passenger seat.

Rodgers eyes were locked on the banks entrance but he was well aware of the conversation going on to the side of him. Immediately after the midnight skin toned man hung up the phone, he questioned Rodgers.

"Aye mon, why FBI only send you? One federal agent?!"

Rodgers didn't answer the man. He sat straight up in the seat and pointed towards the bank. MZ Rae was exiting the banks doors carrying two suitcases. She walked casually out to the roundabouts curb. In his thick Caribbean accent the constable yelled.

"That was your chief, he said you're not FBI anymore! You're a rouge agent! This mission is aborted!"

MZ Rae didn't have to wait long, within seconds the cab pulled up beside her. Rodgers looked up and down the street. He saw the constable's two young detectives about to engage and move in on MZ Rae. Rodgers looked on as the cab squealed wheels pulling off. The constable reached up to his shoulder and pressed the button on the side of his walkie-talkie.

"Stand down!" the constable screamed in the speaker.

"What the fuck?" Rodgers said chopping the man in the throat. The mans' hand involuntarily went to his neck, walkie-talkie flying from the man's hand. Rodgers reached for the walkie. He could hear multiple engines roaring. The constable's hand moved swiftly to his pistol on his hip. Rodgers grabbed the man's hand that was wrapped around the guns butt, preventing the uniformed man from removing it from the holster.

"Colonizer, get your filthy hands off me!"

Rodgers tried to steal a quick glance. He saw the cab that Kish was in in pursuit of, a black Fiat.

Rodgers was head butted by the constable. "BAM!" The blow caused Rodgers to see stars, his hand released from the constable's wrist. He made a move for his own silenced automatic that he carried conveniently holstered, loosely below his left peck underneath his suit jacket. Rodgers squeezed the trigger, firing through his jacket. The slug caught the constable directly in the heart. Rodgers picked up the man's walkie-talkie just as the constable was taking his last breath.

"Engage! Engage!" Rodgers said in his best island accent.

He heaved the constable's large corpse over the bench seat. The body thudded heavily as it hit the floor. Rodgers then slid over under the steering wheel and sped off.

CHAPTER 17

Cash In

Smoke rose from the cobblestone street on the historic side of Georgetown, the capital of the Cayman Islands. Kush stomped on the Fiats gas paddle; the tires screeched.

"Kush!" MZ Rae said shocked but relieved, "oh, am I glad to see you."

Kush hunched over the steering wheel, not taking his eyes off the road.

"What was up with your cap?" Kush asked, "why'd it pull off without you?"

He bit down on his lip as he shifted the five-speed like a formula one driver, zigzagging up and down the small colorful streets.

"Oh!" MZ Rae said thinking of the cab driver Terrence. Before she could reply, Kush continued. "And what the fuck you and Isis doing with Kish?"

He repeatedly took right and left turns, down and up shifting through the crowded streets. "Kish showed up last night."

MZ Rae said frowning her face as she thought, *"Isis must've come when I was in the bank,"* she said to herself.

Within three minutes, Kush was pulling the Fiat into an enclosed motel. The motels car entrance was like that of a drive thru. Once over the small speed hump, the cottage style rooms were encircled.

"Kish ain't right!" Kush said as he whipped the small car around and backed in beside an old VW van. "They were gonna jack you for this money and probably kill your ass!" Kush said looking directly at MZ Rae.

She shook her head trying to figure out what was going on and what just happened. "Terrence must've heard of them!" she said sounding shocked, "that's why he pulled off…to protect me." Her words faded.

MZ Rae gasped when she looked up to see Kush pointing a Russian Ruger .22 at her.

Getting protection was the first objective for Kush when he arrived on the island. While Lana and Sista Vic were getting the lodging, Kush walked until he came upon a strip where illicit gains were being made. He followed the destination of the frequent trail of fiends, going to and fro until he came to the source. That same taped up burner Kush had copped off a fourteen-year-old, chubby Dominican boy the night before, he now aimed at MZ Rae. He aggressively snatched the suitcases that were taking up the whole floor space in between MZ Rae's legs, making her sit awkwardly.

"You working with Kish!" Kush growled.

She shielded her face from the guns deadly stare. "Fuck Kush!" MZ Rae said. "What are you doing? What are you talking about?"

Kush stared at MZ Rae. Her classy squeaky-clean corporate image didn't sway Kush one way or another on whether he believed her. He believed the authenticity of her voice and eyes. But he still held the pistols aim on her.

Kush said flatly, "Kish is a Fed, been planted from day one."

MZ Rae lowered her hands and her expression read disappointment. She chuckled lightly, thinking of the night before and the intimacy with Kish. Suddenly all the weird questions about the Family's next moves and Kish telling her not to call Lana started to add up.

In surprisingly incorrect English, MZ Rae said with authority, "I ain't no Fed, Negro! And I most definitely ain't working with nobody tryna take my share!" She snatched one of the suitcases back from Kush. He lowered the pistol flashing an apologetic smile.

"Sorry, had to be sure," Kush said shrugging his shoulders, "come on, Lana and Sista Vic are inside."

Terrence sped off just as Kish was opening the cab's door for MZ Rae to enter. He didn't know what else to do. While waiting on MZ Rae to return from inside the bank, another beautiful American young lady entered his cab. Her and the lady that he picked up with MZ Rae talked quietly in hushed tones. From peeking in his rear-view Terrence saw anxious, deceptive eyes and tense body language from his two occupants. One of the ladies' hands was stuck inside her purse that rested on her lap. Ever since that, Terrence's instincts screamed out that something wasn't right and that the sweet woman that he had met just seven days ago was in grave danger.

"ERRRRRR!" Terrence's cab peeled from the curb leaving MZ Rae. Kish pulled out a small pistol from her Michael Kors pocketbook and pointed at Terrence's head. The heavy cab screeched to a halt. Isis smacked the dread upside the head.

"Back the fuck up!" She demanded him. But before Terrence could put the cab in reverse, through his rearview, he saw MZ Rae jumping inside a little black and red car. The small Fiat shot around and passed the stopped cab. By the time Terrence threw the gear back into drive, another car he quickly identified as "Babylon" pulled out in front of his cab. Isis took the gun from Kish then swung it at the dreds head. The blow knocked

Terrence's red, black and green crochet hat off.

"Go around them! Follow that car!" Isis and Kish both yelled.

Terrence swerved around the old unmarked Ford. The cab's two left wheels hopped and rode the curb until it cleared its roadblock. With the cold steel pressed firmly to the back of his head Terrence followed every directive Isis and Kish ordered.

"Left...Right…Left..."

No matter what direction they turned in or street they looked down the red and black Fiat wasn't in sight.

"Hold on," Kish said pulling out her phone.

The cab was stopped at a stop sign at a four-way intersection. Traffic in the back of them blew their horns for the cab to go, as Kish swiped and pressed on her phone.

"Her smart ass don't know that iPhones can be tracked!" Kish's phone beeped as she continued, "Come on, they stopped a couple streets over," she said opening the cabs door, "we can walk from here."

Isis gave a nudge to the back of Terrence's head with the pistol before getting out of the cab.

"Qwen get, blood clot!" She gave the pistol back to Kish then threw some bills on Terrence's lap.

"Let's get our money," Isis said to Kish as they crossed the road.

Terrence watched the two women walk hurriedly, both looking down at Kish's phone. He turned directly into a tiki-style bar's parking lot and jumped out. Terrence headed in the direction Isis and Kish went in. He followed the two successfully without being detected. Through a couple alleys and side streets, he stalked cautiously.

When Isis and Kush made their way through a park, that consisted of shady trees, concrete benches and chess tables, Terrence sat at an unoccupied chess bench and watched intently. The ladies didn't look back once as they entered under the motel's wooden pastel colored archway.

CHAPTER 18

La Costa Nostra

At the same time in the northeast of the United States, Coco and X entered an elevator in a Dewey Beach condo. The two of them wore Johnny Janosik uniforms and hats. They carried with them a green leather recliner. Mrs. Mangeni, along with her two sons, carried thick beach towels and sported swim wear as they exited the condo at 11 a.m. Just as Geegee said they would. Every morning the three of them always got an early start on hitting the waves. Salvator Mangeni, those that loved him called him Big Sally and the people that hated or feared him called him The Butcher. Mangeni's first legitimate business was a meat storage and cuttery in Hell's Kitchen. Countless mob affiliates were rumored to have met their demise in that warehouse, by The Butcher's hand. Allegedly, The Butcher fancied running wise guy's body parts through the ten-inch blade while they were still alive.

Big Sal's chauffeur and sole bodyguard was a former New York Jet offensive tackle. Ricardo Rosi, nicknamed Double R. The six foot four, two-hundred-and-eighty-pound brute, left Big Sal out on the thirtieth-floor balcony to answer the knock at the door. Double R's red Pumas had white strips; his matching red pants also had the white strips down the seams. Double R's wife beater fit snug against his barrel chest and solid stomach. He snatched off the white beach towel draped over his neck as he approached the door. Double R's 9-millimeter Barretta, with the six-inch screw-in silencer never parted him, anytime. It was always in one or two places, his hand or stuck in the waistline.

"Who is it?" The fifty something Sicilian called out as he concealed the 9-millimeter pistol inside the towel; he saw two uniformed men when he looked through the peep hole.

"Its Johnnies!" X said sounding timid and unsure, "is a Mrs. Mangeni here?"

Opening the door until the chain stopped it, Double R asked, "What do you's want?"

X and Coco both looked down at the chair that sat on the floor between them. "We have an order for delivery to a….Mrs..." X looked down at a clip board in his hands. "A Mrs. Mangeni. For a green leather comforter."

Double R slammed the door shut. Coco and X looked at one another and hunched their shoulders. Coco wouldn't dare say a word to let the Mad Man hear his thick New York accent. When the door swung opened two Italians stood before X and Coco. It would have been plain to distinguish the two for X, even if Geegee hadn't given him a full description of The Brain, Big Sal and the Braun, Double R. Sally stood at 5'' 9', clearly shorter than his Sasquatch of a bodyguard. But the man's presence was bigger than the three men combined. He wore an ivory linen applejacks cap with matching shirt and polo shorts. Big Sally's pale white feet were in some thong Tommy Hill flip flops.

"What the fuck did she order NOW?!" Sally asked rhetorically, already seeing the comforter.

X nor Coco were naive to the way the boss' bodyguard held and pointed a wrapped up plush white towel at them. They both were well aware that a firearm was inside that towel aimed at them, ready to kill. No one moved for a few seconds. Everyone just stared at the man opposite to him.

"Is it gonna grow wings and fly in here or are you two mullies gonna bring it in."

Sally took a puff off of a G Pin he held in his hand then, passed it to Double R. Coco recognized the flavor as Honey Suckle. The THC infused vape pin looked tiny in between Double R's huge sausage fingers as he held it to his lips. He pressed the button on the side of the gadget then inhaled.

X and Coco both bent down on each side of the chair to lift it. Sally and Double R both backed up two steps letting X and Coco know that they could come no further. Just as Coco and X sat the chair down inside the condos door, Double R had a short spasm of coughs. The sweet but potent liquid THC tasted good, which made it easy to inhale deeper and take harder pulls. Double R was hacking from his misjudged intake, causing his toweled hand to lower. Both X and Coco dropped to one knee before removing their hands from underneath the comforter. A split second later both of their hands appeared holding small caliber pistols. Double R's reaction was fast. The G pins glass valve shattered as Double R dropped it. The white towel dropped from around his hand revealing the silenced nine-millimeter Barretta.

"Pap-Pap-Pap…Pap!" Coco's .22 Bullets dotted Double R's keg of a chest and midsection. X closed the door.

The big man took a step back then fell to his knees. Double R gave one last attempt to raise his pistol.

"Pap!" Coco shot the already teetering man in the center of his forehead, causing the heavy body to crash to the teak wood floor.

"You dumb fucks! Do you know who the fuck I AM?!" Big Sally said not surprisingly without fear.

"SHSSSSH!" X said pointing his pistol at Big Sally while covering his lips with his finger.

X nodded his head to Coco. Coco pulled out a flip phone and pressed send. The room was silent as the call was placed on speaker. They listened as it rang on the other line.

"Hello?" A voice said from the speaker.

"Mangeni's a memory," Coco replied back into the phone.

When Sally heard Geegee's distinctive voice coming from the phone he closed his eyes and shook his head.

"Excellent," Geegee said, "I'll meet you at your boat in about an hour. I have a bonus for ya for the great job."

CHAPTER 19

Love of da Money

Kush and MZ Rae each carried one of the heavy cash filled suitcases as he led her to room 302. Before Kush gave a light drum roll knock to the door, he told MZ Rae that Lana's mother had been killed. MZ Rae's heart sank. Tears started to well up in her eyes within the seconds it took for the door to swing open. MZ Rae embraced Lana as soon as she entered the small, shabby motel room. She cried as she hugged Lana tight, wishing she could take her friend's pain away. As the two friends cried on one another's shoulders, Kush took the suitcase MZ Rae was carrying.

"I'm going in the other room with Sista Vic to split this up."

He took both cases and went out the back-sliding door. Two doors down they had another room. It was always an unwritten rule when you were doing dirt in hotels or motels to have multiple rooms.

Lana's bright and cheerful colors that she wore, clashed with her depressing dark mood. Big shades covered her red, puffy eyes. Dried streaks of tears ran from below the glasses down to her red lip stick. Although she was under heavy stress, Lana dressed in relaxing beach attire. Lana's yellow sun hat shaded most of her face. Her auburn colored ponytail hung to the nape of her neck. She wore a yellow wide-necked, loose shirt with C Mack's Lightning in a bottle logo on the front. The long shirt partially covered her form-fitting, white shorts that stopped halfway up her thigh. MZ Rae noticed right away that Lana wasn't acting all herself, even under the circumstances. Lana's words were slurred and her fingers never stopped moving. The tips twitched as Lana repeatedly rubbed her thumbs in a circular motion across the rest of her fingers. Lana abruptly released MZ Rae then sat in one of the two bamboo chairs at the small round table. The only other pieces of furniture were a full-size bed, dresser with a bulky TV resting on it. Lana just stared in the direction of the blank TV screen, as if it were cut on.

"Lana!" MZ Rae yelled.

A slight tinged of fright and fear shot through MZ Rae. She looked on puzzled by Lana's rigid disposition.

"Lana, how you feeling, Girl?" MZ Rae asked walking towards the seated Lana.

Her whole body was still as a statue accept her twitching fingers. MZ Rae pulled Lana's glasses off of her face. She wanted to look into her eyes. Lana's eyes stared straight ahead, through MZ Rae. She grabbed Lana's hands, shaking and squeezing them firmly calling out. She looked desperately in Lana's eyes for any sign of comprehension.

"LANA! LANA!" Lana was unresponsive to MZ Rae's pleading calls.

She didn't move a muscle until hearing the Family's secret knock at the door. Lana jumped and made a B line straight to the door. Before MZ Rae could react and grab Lana or even protest verbally against opening the door, it was open. Isis walked in first followed by Kish. Lana returned back to her seat continuing her previous state of obliviousness. There was a stand-off between MZ Rae, Kish, and Isis.

"Bitch! You the Feds?" MZ Rae said to Kish with a scowl of disgust on her face.

"Shut up ho!" Kish shot back.

"Where's our MONEY?" Isis asked flatly.

Lana sat bolt upright in the chair.

"You rolling with the Feds…and jacking the ONLY people that ever LOVED YOU!"

Lana's former spaced out and absentminded trance was gone, now she showed aggression and acute awareness. She shot to her feet and stood beside MZ Rae.

"Where's the fucking MONEY!" Kish said raising her voice along with a small caliber pistol. She pointed the gun at Lana, "I'm not gonna ask you no more Kalana!" Kish said cocking the gun.

"HOL-HOLD on Kish," Isis said turning to Kish. In a lowered voice Isis said, "This Lana, you not serious. You can't shoot her?" Kish's brow creased as she frowned while giving Isis the evil eye.

"Move out the way, Isis," Kish said through gritted teeth, "over six million!" she said reminding Isis what was at stake.

Isis perched her lips and gave a slight nod. Suddenly and swiftly Isis reached out grabbing Kish's hand holding the pistol. Isis had both of her hands over Kish's hands that were clutching the .38 special. With Kish having more control of the gun she swung her arms to the left and down. She hip tossed Isis and both the women fell to the floor. Lana grabbed MZ Rae's arm and pulled her back away from the tussling women.

"Bitch!" Isis spat.

"POW!"

No one moved or breathed for the seconds of dead silence that followed the gun shot. Kish rolled Isis limp body off of her and sprang to her feet. Out of breath and winded Kish again trained the pistol on Lana and MZ Rae.

"Money…Where da MONEY!"

"Bumbaclot!" Terrence, the cab driver, said at seeing one of the motel's room doors close as he entered the semi-circular structure.

Staying close to the walls Terrence made his way around to Room 302. He stood to the left side of the door trying to listen to the voices from within.

"POW!" The sound of the gun shot forced Terrence to make a move, now.

He didn't even check to see if the door was unlocked, he just delivered a massive kick to the left of the doorknob.

"BOOM!" The door flew open.

Terrence's eyes and mind took only milli-seconds to read and comprehend what was happening and what must be done. Before Kish could turn around fully to see what was happening Terrence was already upon her. Terrence swung with all his might at Kish's head catching her with a hard over hand right. The blow struck Kish's temple, knocking over the small table. Lana ran over to Isis while Terrence retrieved the gun. He peeled an unconscious Kish's limp fingers from around the pistol.

Lana cradled Isis's head in the crook of her arm. The single shot had hit Isis just below her left breast. Blood quickly spread and saturated Isis' pink blouse.

"Ice, hold on Baby." Isis last words before breathing her final breath of air were, "I'm sorry…"

MZ Rae ran over to Terrence and hugged the tall dread head.

"You came for me?!" she said in his ear.

"Oh shit! What the Fuck!" Kush said as he led Sista Vic in the room through the back-sliding door.

"Lana get up," Kush spat, "she chose her side!" He helped Lana to her feet.

"Who dat?" Kush said looking at Terrence.

MZ Rae stood on front of the big Rasta. "He's with me," she said confidently.

"Okay, now," Kush said smiling holding his hands up in submission. He held two knapsack bags with drawstrings in each of his hands.

"Look," Kush continued, "here's your share."

He handed one of the black bags to MZ Rae then he turned to Lana, "Queen B, this yours."

Handing Lana one of the bags; he held up the remaining two bags, "I have mines and X's and Sista Vic has hers and Icy Bezel's.

Kush put his arm over Lana's shoulder and his other over Sista Vic's. "Come here," he said to MZ Rae.

Terrence busied himself by tying up Kish with the lamp and clock cords. Sista Vic, Kush, Lana, and MZ Rae formed a small circle, joined together by their arms.

"This is where we all part ways," Kush said looking into each of the ladies eyes, "we are all at this moment officially millionaires. Go anywhere in the world you want except back to the states. I'm pretty sure that there are federal warrants waiting for each one of us back there."

All the lady's shook their heads in agreement.

"Family Love!" Kush said as he backpedaled to the back door, placing his fist over his heart.

Lana hugged Sista Vic and MZ Rae.

"Take care of my sister," she said to Terrence.

Then Lana hurried out the back door after Kush. Sista Vic, MZ Rae, and Terrence exited right behind Lana, leaving an unconscious Kish bound and gagged.

"I don't know where to go or what to do with myself," Sista Vic said to MZ Rae down the alley behind the motel.

MZ Rae stopped and grabbed both of the older woman's hands.

"Go anywhere you want! What's the one place you've always told yourself you would go if you ever had the chance?" Sista Vic thought for a second.

"HMM…Venice, Italy!"

MZ Rae repeated, "Venice!" she looked at Terrence, "Venice?"

Terrence replied, "Irie."

George Rodgers heard off the deceased inspector's radio as he drove up and down the small streets, that a gun shot was called in at a nearby motel. Rodgers pulled into the enclosed motel.

After flashing his badge to the motel's manager Rodger asked, "What room are the Americans in?"

He was given the keys to two rooms, 410 and 302. The former agent didn't waste any time, he pulled out his .45 and cocked it as he walked out of the reception area. Rodgers didn't bother with the keys, the first door he reached was 410.

"Boom!" The door flew wide open.

"Fuck!" Rodgers said at seeing the room was empty.

He continued down the sidewalk passing rooms until he reached 302. He exhaled with his back against the wall and his pistol pointed to the ground before attempting to kick open the door. Just before he was about to make his move he checked to see if the door was locked. It wasn't. Rodgers opened the door slowly.

"My, My, My!" Rodgers said looking down at Kish bound and gagged starring up at him.

He squatted down, grabbed Kish under her arms then propped her up against the bed. Rodgers removed the gag.

"Untie me!" Kish demanded.

Rodgers laughed. "I can't do that sweetie," he said standing up.

He pulled one of the chairs up and sat close to Kish while punching in a number on a flip phone.

"You gonna send me to prison, Uncle G?" Kish asked nervously.

Rodgers shook his head. "No, something more deserving."

A few moments later Rodgers spoke into the phone, "Yeah, I do have good news. I have the culprit right here responsible for your nephew's tragic death." Kish's eyes grew large from disbelief and shock.

"Who's that?" Kish asked, her voice trembled and cracked with fear.

Rodgers ignored Kish's questions. "Yes, I can do that for you," Rodgers said into the phone, his eyes darted to Kish momentarily, "o.k. Don Francisco, see you in a few days and I'll bring you proof."

Rodgers closed the phone and let out a deep sigh, "SWEESSH!"

Kish's head and eyes followed Rodgers as he stood up. "Please, Unc. You don't have to do this!"

Rodgers pulled off his belt then kneeled down beside her. With her hands tied behind her back Kish could only squirm, giving little resistance to Rodgers powerful hands. Kish's cries for help were suppressed to inaudible whimpers, once Rodgers had the leather belt around her neck. A single tear ran down his face as he squeezed with all his strength until Kish lay lifeless.

CHAPTER 20

Back to Clara Lee

X could see how Big Sal Mangeni was the boss. The man didn't bust a sweat through the whole ordeal. X thought, *"Ether Sal has one hell of a poker face or he had balls of steel."* X figured the latter.

He wasn't shaken or rattled by the murder of his best friend Double R, or even baffled by the change of plans by the two would be assassins who came to kill him. X felt and saw the general appreciation in Sal's eyes and by the firm hand shake he gave him and Coco.

"Thank you, Pizons…Thank you!" Sal said to X and Coco. He continued to speak in his thick South Bronx accent, "yous' know that that extra bonus Geegee's talking 'bout is a bullet in both yous' heads uh?" Coco and X looked at each other.

"Yeah, we figured that," Coco said, "that's why we didn't murk you."

Big Sal shook his head cracking a smile. "I see you two are fond of chess not checkers. Let's go, I'm going back with you guys."

Sal kissed his fingers then made the sign of the cross over Double R's corpse. He opened the door as X and Coco picked up the comforter they had come with.

As they all walked out Sal said, "Pizons!" Both Coco and X's looked at the dark Sicilian, "don't worry about nothing. You two are now UNTOUCHABLE!"

Evita and Ximena took off in Hector's private DR Airlines jet to the United States within the same hour. They arrived at Salisbury, Maryland's Regional Airport three hours later. Evita's only luggage was a carry-on containing fifty thousand dollars and filled with Ximena's clothes, diapers and toys. She had another twenty grand in her Michel Kors' pocketbook. Evita went to the last Customs Agent on the right just as Fame had instructed when she walked into the airport. She held Ximena while the agent opened her suitcase. The brown skinned man with his hair in waves peered over the top of his glasses at Evita. His name tag read Harlee.

"How long you going to be here in the States?" Evita played along with the small talk.

"Only for three days," she said with a smile swaying her body and the baby slightly from side to side.

Harlee zipped her suitcase back up and stamped Evita's passport.

"Welcome back to America."

"You bout to meet your real da-da. Say Da-da," Evita said to the baby.

The Uber that Evita called just as they landed pulled up while she was giving Ximena kisses. Evita and the driver greeted one another properly. Evita told the Uber driver; whose name was Maxine their destination.

"The Seaford Marina in Blades Delaware."

Although Maxine asked and said all the pleasantries for the occasion, which was a cab ride, Evita still sensed her sadness. Evita felt and saw enough body language to know Maxine was a troubled person. After the cordial introductions they rode in silence. Besides Ximena's baby talk all Evita heard was Maxine's sniffles.

Evita tried to spark up a conversation with Maxine. "Are you from Maryland? Do you have kids? How are you doing today?"

All Evita's questions were answered with one-word responses. Finally Evita lost her patience with trying to talk to the Uber driver.

"What's wrong Maxine?"

"Nothing!" the bushy haired driver replied.

Evita continued, "You can talk to me. Its' obvious that something is bothering you."

"You don't know me," Maxine said then turned on the radio.

Evita kept speaking over a Cardi B song. *"That's the best part, you don't know me from the man in the moon and probably will never see me again. Go ahead and vent, you'll feel a lot better, if you talk about it."*

For the first time, Maxine made eye contact with Evita through the rear view mirror. Evita saw the girls watery red eyes.

"Alright," Maxine said turning the radio off. After taking a deep breath Maxine spoke.

"About a year ago I got this crazy ideal to open up a bookstore in a minority community. Encouraging reading to Black youths as well as the adults," Maxine paused to take another deep breath then continued, "to make a long story short last week I got a letter from the Small Business Association that they were cutting off my financial assistance!"

Evita frowned. "For what?" she asked.

Maxine wiped away tears as she drove across the Maryland/Delaware line. "They said that the new governor was shutting off their minority program!"

Evita touched the stranger's shoulder for comfort. Maxine cried openly now. "The store is a success," she said, "I was just starting to see a profit...plus the community's embracing it!" Evita shook her head.

"My savings are gone and today the builder owner calls and tells me that it's a breach of contract, since the governments aid didn't last twelve months!"

Evita shook her head, "MMM, MMM, MMM!"

Five minutes later Maxine pulled the van into the Seaford Marina. She rode around all the boats that were dry docked until she reached the river's side.

"There she is!" Evita pointed from the back seat at seeing The Clara Lee stenciled in gold and black cursive letters on the back of the big yacht.

"You're about to meet your daddy." Evita squealed squeezing Ximena.

The baby reacted with giggles from her mom's excited and happy energy.

"How much do I owe you?" Evita asked Maxine as she exited the van.

She pulled her carry on out and held the baby as she approached Maxine's door.

"That'll be 50 dollars," Maxine said when her window was down.

"Feel better?" Evita asked.

"Huh?" Maxine replied confused.

"With venting," Evita said, "getting that weight off of your shoulders."

Maxine smiled, "Yes. A little."

Evita released the handle of her carry on then reached into the van and grabbed Maxine's hand.

"Keep pushing and never give up on your dreams!" Evita said squeezing her hand and looking Maxine in her red eyes. "I left the fare in the back seat. Goodbye and good luck."

Maxine turned instantly to look for the money in her back seat. The lady was nice and all but Maxine didn't trust her enough not to question the lady's odd ploy of not handing the money to her. Maxine gasped and grabbed her chest at what saw. She silently prayed to herself as she reached out to touch it.

"Please GOD, don't let this be a dream."

As Evita walked towards the Clara Lee she heard Maxine scream and the vans door open. Before Evita could fully turned around to look back Maxine was upon her. She wrapped her arms around Evita and the baby.

"Thank you! Thank you! Thank you!" Maxine said with tears of joy streaming down her cheeks.

Evita had left a bundle of cash on the Uber driver's seat in the amount of ten thousand dollars.

"You're welcome," Evita said struggling to breathe from the bear hug Maxine was applying.

After Evita was free from Maxine's tight embrace, she spoke to the jubilant Uber driver.

"I don't think it was a coincident that our paths crossed," Evita said wiping a single tear from her eye.

Maxine shook her free hand repeatedly and even kissed it a few times.

"Bless you...Bless you!" Maxine cried. She blew kisses to Evita with the stack of bills over her heart as she backpedaled to the van.

Evita let out a sigh of blessings and pleasure as she watched Maxine pull off. That was the first time she had ever given anybody anything let alone a complete stranger and MONEY. The feelings that she felt were a climax only rivaled by X's touch. Evita's chest swelled with pride.

"That felt good," she cooed to Mena, kissing the baby's neck. Just as she spun around and grabbed the carry-on's tall handle a voice startled her.

"Hello, Beautiful!"

Coco, X, and Sal watched the Seaford Marina from across the Nanticoke River. A drawbridge lay where the river narrowed. They had a clear view of the Clara Lee from the third floor's outside walkway of the Lake View Condos.

"They're in there," Sal said 15 minutes into their surveillance of the Clara Lee. No one had come to the yacht nor was there any movement aboard.

"You sure?" Coco questioned.

Not accustomed to being questioned Sal gave Coco a sarcastic look. "I'm positive," Sal said confidently.

It was high tide and the river's choppy waters looked gray on the overcast day.

"Geegees disloyal ass is in there, along with his right-hand man The Pug. He would have been his Underboss," Sal chuckled before he continued, "if you two didn't spare my life. But anyway." He waved his hand. "They have to erase anything and anyone that tie them to whacking a boss!"

Coco shook his head in agreement finishing Sal's sentence. "So to ensure without a shadow of a doubt that we're dead and silent they gonna do it personally!"

"Howboutit!" Sal stated.

"Look!" X said.

A van rode slowly around the marina, it stopped at the edge of the parking lot. The van pulled as close as it could to the docks where the

Clara Lee lay tied and anchored. A tugboats horn blew in the background as the three men watched a lady get out of the van carrying a baby. X's jaw dropped as he squinted his eyes. The draw bridge began to raise. Lights on each side of the bridge turned red while a crossing barrier came down stopping the flow of traffic. The tugboat preceded slowly towards the bay. The raised bridge blocked their view of the woman, but X knew at first sight who the lady was.

"What the fuck?!" X took off toward the steps to go down.

"HOL-HOLD UP Sun!" Coco said grabbing X's arm.

Sal yanked on X's other arm.

"Look! Look! The Pug!" Sal said pointing. Standing on the starboard of the Clara Lee a man appeared.

The three men could only see the back of Pug, but it was clear that he was talking to Evita who they still couldn't see because of the raised bridge. Once the tugboat finally cleared, the drawbridge slowly began its descend. It wasn't until the bridge was lowered completely that Evita, with baby in tow could be seen boarding the Clara Lee. X's heart felt as if it exploded in his chest at laying eyes on his baby girl for the first time and the love of his life walking into a lion's den. Coco and Sal had to restrain X a second time as he tried to plow his way through them, fuming with rage.

"That's my wife and baby! I gotta get down there!" X said anxiously.

"Control your emotions, Pizon!" Sal hissed, just above a whisper while tightening his grip on X's elbow. Sal continued. "We only gonna get one crack at this. There isn't going to be any do overs."

Coco agreed. "Yeah B, we gotta mastermind this shit or them spaghetti eating muthafuckers gonna kill us all." Coco looked at Sal.

"No offense, Pizon." Sal nodded.

"No offense taken." Both Sal and Coco released X once he had calmed down and relaxed.

The once confident, sure and smooth gangster that Coco had admired for his cool head in the mist of chaos was now a wreck. Coco could see and feel X's pain and distress. It was as if a light had been switched when X had seen Evita and his baby. Coco watched as X's shoulders slumped and eyes watered. That look changed within the minutes it took Sal to quarterback and explain a plan to board the Clara Lee to kill Geegee. X ears listened to Sal but his mind was on his only true love Evita and the most beautiful creature he had ever laid eyes on.

"I wonder what's her name," he thought.

X's heart melted as he visualized the precious baby and Evita, but it hardened quickly with the thought of the mortal danger they were in. By the end of Sal's briefing of how they would comfort the situation, X's attitude went from somber to furious. He couldn't wait to get aboard the yacht and spill the blood of anybody that stood in between him and his family.

"Capisce?" Sal questioned X and Coco.

"Capisce," they both said in unison.

CHAPTER 21

Vigilante

Former U.S. Federal Agent George Rodgers woke up in a cold sweat, disoriented. The dead faces of Kish and the Cayman Island Constable haunted his dreams. Rodgers had killed before but only in the line of duty. These homicides were different, he had murdered in cold blood. He looked around loosening his tie and collar. His face glistened from perspiration. It took him a few seconds to recall that he was aboard a plane. He looked out of his window seat at the top of the velvet looking pearly white and silver clouds. A tall slim middle-aged stewardess walked down the planes isle with a small bag collecting the passengers' trash. She stopped at the row Rodgers sat in. An elderly Hispanic woman had the aisle seat in Rodgers row.

"Is everything alright?"

The tall blonde asked the old lady before she looked over to Rodgers. The stewardess gave him a quick wink and flashed a smile displaying perfect white teeth. Seeing her face eased Rodgers' nerves a little. He forced a smile that looked more like a grimace.

"I'm good," Rodgers replied. His eyes followed her as she moved on to the next row of passengers.

For a few seconds, Rodgers' mind was free from all the problems that he had created. The once decorated special agent had threw away his prominent and extensive career. Not following his last directive from his superior and breaking protocol by pursuing the Diamond State Mafia was the least of his worries. He had murdered two people.

"What have I done?!" Rodger's thoughts screamed out in his head.

His mind was bombarded with accusing and questioning voices as well as images of an eminent arrest. Looking out of the window into the vast baby blue skies calmed Rodger's anxiety, as he took a few deep breaths.

"I was just trying to get the bad guys!" Rodgers chuckled out loud. Because the voice that he heard was his own but not the manly one he had now. It was the voice he had as a child.

"He was just trying to get the bad guys!" Rodgers said to himself.

That chuckled turned into hearty laugh. He remembered the countless comic book vigilantes he had read of as a child. In those comic books, collateral damage was always done by the hero in an attempt to capture a villain. When they wrecked the city or injured innocent civilians an advocate of the hero would always say something like, "He was just trying to get the bad guy!"

Rodgers continued to stare out the window, past the passing clouds. The picture was so serene. He thought of two of his all-time favorite superhero vigilantes and how they delivered justice. Frank Castle, the Punisher and Bruce Wayne, the Batman. A ray of sunlight peaked over a cloud blinding him momentarily. Since he was thinking of vigilante justice when the celestial omen occurred.

Suddenly he had an epiphany. What he first thought of as a dilemma he now saw as an opportunity or better yet, "a chosen path." All his actions that he had done up to this point became justified in his eyes. As the plane soared over the Gulf of Mexico George Rodgers vowed that he would continue to "get the bad guys." But this time it would be different. Long gone are the days of bureaucratic red tape and the rights of criminals.

"I'm going Judge Dred on you muthfuckers!" Rodgers said to himself before laughing out loud wickedly.

Sounding more like a comic book villain instead of a superhero. The old lady sitting on the end seat looked up from her novel she was reading over to Rodgers.

"Loco gringo!" She spat shaking her head.

Rodgers held a newfound confidence when he exited the plane into the sticky, hot Mexico City atmosphere. He moved with the swagger of a man that knows his purpose. He spotted the Don's henchmen. One was behind the wheel of a jeep with no doors. The other stood beside it and both men wore big Stetsons. A wooden pistol handle was visible, sticking out of the standing Mexican's dungarees.

"Senor Rodgers!"

The short Mexican in a flannel shirt, jeans and cowboy boots greeted him. Rodgers jumped in the back seat. He graciously accepted a bottle of tequila from the driver. He took a modest sized shot from the dusty bottle and frowned. Both the driver and passenger laughed. A mariachi band blasted through the speakers as they sped off. The surroundings went from urban streets to rural dirt roads. Rodgers plotted his next moves in between swigs of tequila.

"Imma get my bank up, along with my hardware and artillery…and build me an army. An army of heroes like myself, all courtesy of the Don!"

CHAPTER 22

Who's the Boss

"Hurry! Hurry! My wife is having a heart attack!" the dispatcher responded back calmly.

"Ok Sir, is your wife still conscious?!" Sal yelled into the cell phone.

"She's in and out Ma'am. We're at the Seaford Marina in my yacht, the Clara Lee. Is somebody on their way?"

"Yes Sir," the dispatcher replied, "Paramedics will be there in less than five minutes." With hearing that, Sal acted as if his wife's situation had turned dire.

"Oh Christ, I have to perform CPR! She stopped breathing!" Sal hung up the phone.

"They're coming," he said to X and Coco, "give me both of your heaters."

Two minutes later, a wailing ambulance pulled into the marina with its lights flashing. When the two medics jumped out of the ambulance to run aboard The Clara Lee, Coco and X were a minute behind them.

"What the fuck is going on?" X and Coco heard Geegee below yelling to the first responders.

"Who's having the heart attack?" asked one of the medics anxiously.

"There's no one having a fucking heart attack here!" the Pug reiterated.

X and Coco made their way down into the yacht's spacious cabin by way of the spiral stairs. Sal's objectives were to disrupt and distract.

"What's up? What's happening?" Coco asked, he and X looked baffled and bewildered at the sight of the paramedics.

"Evita!" X called out, not able to hold back his emotions. She jumped up with the baby in her arms and met X's strides toward her. When they embraced X whispered in her ear.

"Get ready Baby, I love you!"

Geegee was busy assuring the paramedics that they had the wrong boat and that no one here needed any medical attention. It took a few minutes before the two medics were convinced that no one needed their help aboard the yacht. They made their exit. No sooner than the medics turned to make their way up the spiral stairs, The Pug whipped out a big forty-five revolver. He pointed at Coco who was closest to him. Coco held his hands up as the Pug frisked him down.

"Get away from her!" he ordered X as he trained the gun on him and Evita.

"What's up Geegee?" X questioned.

Looking at Geegee for an explanation, "I thought we was cool?"

Geegee just smiled, resembling his deceased father The Slugger as Pug patted down X aggressively.

"You two move over the fuck over," the Pug ordered X and Coco.

He kept the pistol on them as they both sat on a white crush leather sofa. Evita sat in a matching love seat clutching the baby. Tears ran down her face as she stared unblinking into X's eyes. Geegee peeped through a slit in the curtains out of one of the yachts curved windows.

"Alright. They're pulling out," he said to the Pug; the Pug just shook his head.

"What you shaking your big ass head for, whack these mullies!" Geegee spat.

The Pug raised the big gun up slightly aiming for X's head.

"Pow-Pow!"

Two shots rang out from the spiral stair way. Evita gasped and the baby screamed. The Pugs arm dropped as he teetered like the tin man for a full three seconds before toppling over onto the glossy teakwood floor. One shot blew a piece of his skull off and the other hit just below his cerebellum into the Pugs thick neck. Sal moved from the cover of the steps with guns in both hands aimed at Geegee. Geegee's face paled from shock and fright, he was speechless as Big Sal walked towards him.

"You disloyal sack of shit!" Sal said wearing a smile like the joker.

Coco ran into the bedroom to retrieve the money in the two suitcases that X had promised him.

"Help me tie this fucking stinking ass pig up!" Sal said to X who was holding his child for the first time.

Evita cupped his face with trembling hands, crying tears of joy. Coco came from the bedroom grinning. He not only laid eyes on or just touched the million dollars in the cases, Coco rubbed some of the crisp bills across his face and even licked a stack with his tongue. He sang the Million Dollar Man's theme song as he put the two suitcases under the sink's cabinet then returned to join the others.

"Money. Money. Money. Moneeeey!" Coco sang snapping his fingers.

"I got 'em Big Dog," he said to X, "chill with yo' Wiz."

While Coco and Sal used their belts to subdue Geegee, X got acquainted with Evita and his daughter.

"I thought they had took you from me!" Evita said with tears of joy in the eyes. She touched his face gently. Looking at him in awe.

"What's her name?" X asked after giving Evita a slow and intense head to toe look over.

The baby reached for X with outstretched arms. He let her climb into his arms. X held the baby gingerly. Her small hand touched his face like she had seen her mother do then tugged on his beard.

"Her name is Ximena Alethia Watson." X mouthed the baby's whole name to himself.

"Daddy's baby!" Blowing a strawberry on the baby's neck, she giggled.

X turned to Evita licking his lips. "You know I just got out da pen." They kissed, slow passionate kisses turned aggressive and greedily.

"Hey!" Sal said out of breath, "you two will have plenty of time to do that on the cruise up to Jersey." X and Evita looked at keep other. "Unlike this piece of shit." Sal kicked Geegee hard in the face before he continued, "I do have something for you guys. A token of my appreciation. You know…for saving my LIFE."

CHAPTER 23

Bag Your Baggage

The automatic lights flickered on at five a.m. sharp. Dreams of freedom were interrupted by realities of nightmares of being confined, cold and hungry. In the desolate eight by eight cell Icy Bezel was already on his hundredth push up. From the bottom bunk his celly Dito stirred, pulling a thin blanket over his head to block the bright lights.

"You on it early ain't you bro," Dito stated from underneath the covers before sitting up.

He immediately reached for his glasses on the metal shelf above his head. After putting on his designer prescriptions, Dito rubbed his arms.

"Damn its cold in this bitch!"

He slid his socked feet down into the nation's generic reddish-brown commissary flops. Dito then stood up, stretched and yarned before stiff legging it over to the metal toilet to pee. His turned back was the only courtesy he could give his celly.

Icy Bezel just grunted out, "Uuhuh," to Dito's comment as he pushed up and down.

He jumped up from doing his push-ups then looked through the small window in the door, out onto the tier. He didn't turn around until Dito finished peeing.

"What's for breakfast?" Dito asked.

"Some bullshit. Two little ass sausages with oatmeal," Icy Bezel answered.

He breathed hard as he jumped back down on the floor for another set.

"Well, I ain't doing my push-ups," Dito said now brushing his teeth at the push bottom metal sink connected to the toilet. He continued speaking around the toothbrush, "Nigga we going to be hungry as hell eating that little bit of food.

You better conserve that energy!" Icy Bezel just laughed.

"You just don't want to do your set." Dito shook his head.

"You damn right C Rox!" Dito called Icy Bezel by his neighborhood's name.

"Tired of this shit. Hungry all day, losing weight like a muthafucka!" Dito continued as he put on the D.O.C. issued pants with elastic waist and V-neck shirt, "these sorry ass C.O.'s won't even let a brotha get a haircut. Got us going to court and visits looking like starved bums."

Icy Bezel didn't say a word. He was stuck in his own thoughts as he stood in front of the locked steel door. He stared out of the thick glass down at the food cart workers preparing to serve breakfast. It had almost been two months since Icy had been incarcerated. Because of the large quantity of drugs and Icy's record his bail was set at $100,000. The Families lawyer, Michael Brewer, told Icy that he'd be happy if he could get him eight to ten years. Icy Bezel hadn't even planned on doing the fifty days he had been down for already. In his mind Icy banked on the Family "cashing in" down to the Cayman's and then bailing him out. After getting free he would get lost in a distant country in a tropical climate that has no extradition.

Icy Bezel's expectations and hopes went sky high just twenty days into his bid. On that day a correctional officer he had never seen came to break the permanent guard. The heavyset balding officer just curled a finger to Icy who sat watching two people play chess.

"Me?" Icy asked pointing to his own chest.

The C.O. with the handlebar mustache just gave a nod of his head. When Icy Bezel got to the elevated desk the C.O. handed him a single yellow sticky note sheet. It read:

Swing low, sweet chariot,

Coming for to carry me home,

Swing low, sweet chariot,

Coming for to carry me home.

Icy Bezel broke into a wide grin. *"Sista Vic!"* he said to himself.

He and the crew always told Sista Vic that she was their Harriet Tubman, Moses.

"Because when worst comes to worst we can rely on you to get us through." He could see and hear Sista Vic laughing just clear as day.

He was a hundred percent sure that this was a message from The Family. It's a verse from Sweet Chariot, a song that communicated to slaves that Harriet was coming to lead them to freedom. Icy didn't sleep for the first week after receiving the message, anxious to be free and rich. That was nearly a month ago. Icy's anticipation and high hopes of freedom gradually diminished with each passing day since. At this point and time, Icy Bezel only held a small sliver of hope at seeing better days in his immediate future. He had begun to prepare his mind and body for a long jail stint.

After eating breakfast, the inmates were locked back into their cells. Icy bezel and Dito played Tonk for push-ups until lunch at ten. First rec was right after lunch. Inmates bolted out of the doors as soon as the mechanical locks were heard opening. Some ran to the phones, others to the T.V. Eager to get every last second out of the forty-five-minute rec, Icy Bezel sat at one of the stainless-steel tables to play a game of chess. Five minutes into the match with Nick Greasy the telephone on the C.O.'s desk rang. Normally Icy Bezel's ears would be at attention, listening for his name to be called but feeling his chances of making bail were slim, Icy paid it no mind. He was almost in full bid mode. Meaning he would accept his jail time and not squawk, nor let his mind play tricks on him. He wouldn't drive himself mad by holding on to delusional hopes of a life outside the concrete and steel walls.

"Lavander Jones! BAG YOUR BAGGAGE!" The burley C.O. yelled.

Icy Bezel let out a marine's, "Hoo Raa!"

CHAPTER 24

2 Years Later – Better Days

"Man, you gotta be here!" Kush pleaded over the phone to X.

"Bro," X said, "I would love to be there, but..." X stammered, trying to use the right words. "But you know that wouldn't be safe for any of us. It doesn't matter that we're not on U.S soil, it just ain't safe for us to be together in one spot!"

Kush clearly took offense. "What?" Kush spat out. He felt snubbed and brushed off. "You worried about the Feds? Them mothafuckas ain't sweating us." Kush continued, "we've all been legit for over two years Bro! We out of sight, out of mind!"

X let out a grunt, "UGH!" Kush questioned X's gesture.

"What?"

X walked casually through one of his five tobacco slat barns. He picked up one freshly rolled Cuban cigar from a pile of hundreds that were on a long wooden table. Two senior gentlemen sat at opposite ends of the table, hand rolling the tobacco into cigars. Their hands moved sure and fluently, masters of their craft. X lit the flavorful cigar before speaking.

"OUR homie is shoveling MAD dogshit!" Kush couldn't believe his ears.

"Did X just say that Icy Bezel is selling Heroin?" Kush asked himself before saying, "Fuck him, that niggas crazy! His hot ass can't affect us anymore anyway!"

Which was true, none of the family members were wise to any of the others location. The only way they could contact one another was by an old flip throw away phone. Each Family member had a phone. The phones only held the five numbers of the others. Today was the first time in two years that X had heard it ring. Kush continued, "he got a fuckin million dollars and he still selling dope! Greedy ass nigga!"

For about fifteen seconds X's mind drifted off. Oblivious to reality he didn't hear a word that Kush was saying. X had just envisioned his life without Evita and Mena. He would be still robbing, killing or worst dead. X closed his eyes and thanked his ancestors for protecting him.

"Yo! Yo X!" Kush yelled into the phone getting X's attention back. "Lanie would love that shit Bro, I would love for you to be there…and to see you too! I mean…it isn't every day that your best friend and favorite cousin get married."

X remained silent, pondering. He questioned his own loyalty, his lack of emotion and empathy. X asked himself was he wrong over not really wanting to see anyone from his past. For him the past was dark times, far behind them. His life now was vibrant with exactly that LIFE. Living a good life full of love, laughter, and good memories. Whereas in his past life, every day he felt death was near. A thirty-year prison sentence or getting riddled with bullets were the fates of many of their childhood friends. X wasn't ashamed of any of the terrible deeds he had to commit to ensure wealth for him and his family. Nor was he proud of all the pain and despair he had dished out either. He only found gratitude in knowing that his kids would be blessed with wealth and opportunity. They will have all the advantages to succeed in life from his bloody money.

X also was a man who believed in karma. He justified his heinous acts by telling himself his self that he only did bad things to bad people. X has been firmly planted in Cuba since him and his family had arrived. He hadn't thought once about leaving the big island. Life was good. X didn't want to do anything to affect his harmonious life. X's only priorities in life were Evita and Mena. He had no room to love anyone else. All his love was poured into them. X picked one of the safest countries for him and his family to live in peacefully, the proud country of Cuba. He figured hell would freeze over before the Cuban government cooperated with the United States, so the international warrant the FBI had on him didn't apply in Cuba. He knew they would be safe as long as they stayed in Cuba. For the first time in his life, X felt at peace.

Nowadays, X found positive ways to become thrilled and burn adrenaline. His hobbies were high stakes chess matches and mountain climbing. He loved playing the bongos and salsa dancing with Evita. X was a name he hadn't heard in two years, at least out loud. Here he was Yusef. He and Evita had purchased an eighteen-acre prosperous tobacco farm, tucked in a lush valley. A five-bedroom Spanish colonial home came with the buy. The tan-ish and peach colored "big house" sat at the foothills of a lush green mountain. Beyond the mango trees that peppered the property were the vast tobacco fields that stretched out for miles. The whole display was simple and calming. It could be on a poster that read SERENITY. It looked just like it did a century ago.

"Yes. I'll be there bro," X said still sounding unsure of himself.

The second those words were out of his mouth X was thinking twice about his decision. He was happy for Lana and Kush. Especially grateful, but mostly relieved at knowing that Lana was in good hands with Kush. X still thought about and prayed for Lana every day. Introducing Lana to the street life was the one move he wished he could take back. The guilt of

Lana's pain and mental condition weighed heavy on X. He felt that he was the sole reason Lana was "fucked up in the head." More than a few times while thinking of Lana, X shed tears. Out of all the dope dealing, robbing and even killing, ruining Lana's life was his only regret.

X could hear the joy in his oldest friend's voice once he agreed to attend the wedding. He grinned when an image of Kush and his cheesy smile popped into his mind. He was happy for his friend's love and happiness. X knew the feeling.

"Where y'all at?" X asked.

"The Mother Land!" Kush proudly informed X. "Nairobi! The Green city in the sun."

But just as suddenly as the elation of the marriage of his cousin and friend grew on him, another feeling seeped in. Dread. It would be X's first time leaving his safe haven of Cuba since he'd been there. Thoughts of all the bad things that could go wrong once he was out of the country were bombarding him. X's breathing became clipped. He felt as if he was in a small box, a coffin. Sweat rolled down his baldhead and face. X fought to clear his mind and suppress the millions of wicked thoughts. This feeling wasn't foreign to X. In the line of work that included robbery and murder, one's nerves often became strained. X hadn't experienced one of these bouts in over three years. When Lana was raped.

"Senor?" X called to one of the elderly men that were rolling the cigars. "Rum? Where's the rum?" X gestured with his hand like he was taking a drink.

Roberto was one of 10 employees that X had inherited when he brought the business, pickers, hangers, and rollers. Roberto looked and moved good for a 76-year-old man. He spoke little English but knew exactly what "Senor Yusef" was talking about. The old man reached down below the table. Roberto's hand appeared holding a pint of Cuban Rum.

X guzzled a mouth full of the rum whole. The slight tremble in his hands steadied, he began to take deep slow breaths. X knew that it wasn't a coincidence that his anxiety was triggered. Leaving Cuba was a high-risk situation for him. X would be vulnerable to all his worst fears as soon as he steps foot off the island, imprisonment, extortion or assassination. He was rich now, not only in wealth but health and happiness. To protect and keep all he has Yusef the soft-spoken family and businessman would transform into X the gangster. X blinked away his drifting thoughts. He took a light pull from the fresh and perfectly rolled cigar.

"Salute!" X said to Roberto before taking another shot of the sweet beverage. Roberto "saluted" X then took a swig from the bottle as well.

CHAPTER 25

Mole Mules

Rodgers grinned slightly to himself, admiring the behind of the woman walking directly in front of him. Two hours into doing what he called "slithering," Rodgers replaced the man he trailed behind into a woman.

"If I'm gonna have to be staring at the back of someone for hours, might as well make it something with a nice ass!"

He thought to himself, *"Life is fucking great!"*

George Rodgers nowadays was known only as Santini. He adopted the moniker from the renegade airman in the hit TV show Airwolf that he watched as a boy. Santini began as a tiny small voice deep down in Rodgers subconscious. Santini's voice of resistance grew more dominant and profound over the years at seeing firsthand how the scales of justice swayed for the right price or the right people.

For years Rodgers just kept his head down and blinders on to the blatant injustices. He worked hard on each case and assignment. Rodgers life was dedicated to law enforcement. Even as he moved up the structured hierarchy the voice still could be heard. It whispered of rebellion and "true justice." Looking over the week's closed cases one day as an agent, Rodgers noticed a pattern to the convictions, acquittals and dismissals.

Jamal Long-ten ounces of crack cocaine-8 years. George Kosnoski-10 ounces of powder cocaine-five years suspended for 1-year incarceration. Daniel Winston-tier 5 pedophile-3 years suspended for 10 years' probation.

Not only did his inner voice that screamed hypocrisy grow louder, Rodgers developed a mentality of a lynch mob. He could and would fix the wrongs of the broken judicial system, by any means necessary. The self-proclaimed 'super-agent' felt guilty and coward like for not taking action against evil. Today looking back, he recognized that voice. That feeling. That gnawing, at the truth, was his God-given conscience.

"The truth is supposed to be irrefutable." Rodgers said to himself fifteen years into being a G Man.

After witnessing a Catholic priest get acquitted of molesting ten teenage boys Rodgers had had enough. "The system is a joke. A fucking big game!" Rodger's last thread of pride for being a lawman disappeared.

"The elite, the privileged, rich and powerful are all living a lie."

The voice of awareness and righteousness echoed in Rodger's head, no longer suppressed by the sense of entitlement and propaganda of the United States. He could no longer ignore the corruption and the atrocities of the government and its so-called protectors. Rodgers had seen child predators and rapists go free while low level drug dealers get sentenced to five to 10 years in a State or Federal Penitentiary.

The alter ego of Santini blossomed the day that the once decorated Special Agent George Glenn Rodgers murdered the Cayman Island constable and Kish. He was now on the FEDS Blacklist, as a wanted man. Over the past two years Santini had amassed a fortune for himself and had become a major asset to the Mexican Cartel's Don Franciso Rameriz. Whatever job the Don delegated down, whether big or small, subtle and clean or loud and dirty, Santini and his men executed it down to a "T". From extortion, transporting various cargo to assassination, nothing was off limits to Santini except causing harm to civilians. Any opportunity he got to eradicate what he called "Real Bad Men" off the face of the earth, he did. When he wasn't doing jobs for the Don, Santini preyed upon these "Real Bad Men." Rapist, killers, and corporate embezzlers were his main focus but any undesirable committing criminal acts could feel his wrath. Rodgers or rather Santini relished and took pride in his new role of being the 'boogie man' to the real bad men. He castrated all pedophiles before watching them die slow deaths. The "Real Bad Men" that Santini murdered, he never took a dime from them. He wasn't doing it for the money. He was Karma to the ones that were too slippery for conviction in the court of law. At least that's how Santini felt. He looked at it like it was his duty and pleasure. His very own contribution to making the world a better place.

"Mucho beautiful but uh...perezoso," Rodgers said in his best Spanish to the woman walking in front of him.

The Honduran woman in her late twenties looked back and patted her behind. Rodgers laughed out loud, his mind instantly picturing the attractive lady buck naked and underneath him. She had been complaining that her back and legs were hurting for hours. He was aroused as he watched her toned buttocks shift from side to side. She wore tan Capris, her brown calves glistened from sweat.

"And we HAVE a WINNER!" Rodgers said to himself.

Once every month Rodgers and his men did this excursion. He nicknamed it "slithering" because they moved undetected underground. Literally right under the authority's noses. Each time Santini and his men ravished any senorita of their choice that were in the lineup for the journey.

Today along with Rodgers were his two men the brothers Mack and

Truck. Mack lead the line while Truck was about 20 feet behind. Rodgers was the very last of the group. The three of them were armed. They guided ten Hispanics, six females and four males. The Hispanics ranged in age from early twenties to mid-fifties. They all were fleeing from different forms of oppression, from various countries of South and Central America. The ten civilians each carried on their backs big camping style bookbags. The small convoy trooped through the dimly lit underground tunnel. The tunnel was three feet in width and five feet high. The simple but sophisticated tunnel had electricity, water pumps and ventilation. Rodgers and his mercenaries' primary objective was to make sure the cargo that the refugees carried made it across the border.

Santini and his men carried automatic pistols and semi-automatic rifles for insurance. Each of the illegals were paid a hundred dollars and free passage to the land of the free and home of the brave. All the determined souls had to do was trek three days underground from Mexico to Arizona to deliver ten kilos each. There was never a shortage of participants willing to take the risk and get into the United States. In the twenty-second hour of the second day Rodgers received a text.

"*!" Rodgers immediately text back "/".

He received another text. "!"

"For Christ sake Joey!" Rodgers said out loud as he pulled out another phone from his fatigues.

He was calling Joseph Thomas. Joe was Rodgers friend. They had formed a bond when Rodgers came through the academy. Their friendship had lasted over the years, even after Rodgers became a wanted man. Just like when they were fellow agents, they still exchanged information back and forth to one another.

"The GREAT Santini!" Joey said loud into the phone with a chuckle.

"What the fuck is so important that can't wait," Rodgers said to his friend.

"Hey you son-of-a-bitch…I love ya!" Joey slurred.

Rodger laughed, "What you want old man. You been drinking?"

"And smoking reefer!" Joe Thomas said. He continued, "I got something for you."

"What?" Rodgers replied.

Joey shot back, "It's WHO!"

"Well, who is it?" Rodgers asked shaking his head.

"Lavander Jones!" Joey said, "he popped back up on our radar about two months back."

Rodgers knew that eventually he would get his chance to come face to face again with the Diamond State Mafia and deliver justice. The wait was over. Santini stopped in his tracks.

"Where is he?"

Agent Thomas replied. "He's in Cape Verde."

A sly grin stretched across Santini's face. "CAPE VERDE!"

"Yes," Joey continued, "Mr. Icy's allegedly responsible for the distribution of metric tons of pure opium…"

CHAPTER 26

International Playboy

Off of the coast of West Africa lay Tortuga. One of several islands that made up the Island nation of Cape Verde. This is where Icy Bezel made his home. He invested his money into windmills. Cape Verde is famous for its strong winds that either come from the coast of Africa or the vast Atlantic Ocean. The natural energy of the windmills brought power, along with work for the people of the Islands. Clean cheap energy and jobs were great for the Cape Verdeans but what was even better was that Icy Bezel was of African descent. That he wasn't an outside colonizer exploiting them or their land. For that fact the people loved and cherished Icy Bezel. He was adopted as one of their own for contributing to the country's growth and forwardness. Recognized by the politicians down to the peasant winos.

Icy Bezel's house was unconventionally shaped. It went up in a forty-five-degree angle with Icy Bezel's room at the house's highest peak. His bedroom extending out to an open terrace that faced the Motherland. Only 354 miles of the Atlantic Ocean separate them. The eight-bedroom palace of pleasure was said to have been first built in sixth century by Hanno the Navigator, the Carthaginian. The architecture style was Portuguese Kriol.

Icy lived every moment of life to the fullest and demanded the best out of it. He was a rare breed of man that had lived in every caste or class system. He had lived in poverty and he'd been wealthy. But now he was filthy rich and felt free as a bird. After being in prison caged like a beast Icy developed a newfound respect for nature. He now wanted to be outside in the fresh air absorbing nature as much as he could. Icy had built a glass ceiling over his bedroom. The huge room extended to an open terrace, located at the house's highest point. At four a.m., a full moon shone down on Icy Bezel and the two women that shared his bed. A gentle breeze blew through the long Kente patterned silk curtains, onto the three naked bodies. Rondigas, an old childhood friend that died in Icy's arms visited him in his dreams this night.

"YOU SLIPPING!" Rondigas screamed to Icy.

Icy Bezel jumped up sitting upright as he woke up abruptly. The two Portuguese African descent women stirred a little but still lay sound asleep as Icy eased out of bed.

"It's not there," a voice said startling Icy as he was just about to reach for the drawer of his nightstand.

"What the fuck?" Icy Bezel said while peering at the dark corner the voice came from.

Two red beams appeared aiming at his chest.

"OOO!" Icy said raising his hands to the sky, "y'all could at least of left my pistol and gave me a fucking fighting chance!"

A tall figure stepped from the room's dark corner where the moonlight didn't reach. The infrared beams remained trained on Icy as the unknown man stopped five feet from him.

"You don't HAVE to die today Mr. Icy," Santini said as he pulled the ghost face off revealing his face to Icy Bezel.

"What the fuck you want and who the fuck are you?" Icy asked.

He pointed to an ash tray on the nightstand that held a fat spliff. Icy slowly reached out to pick up the fat joint of marijuana and lighter from the nightstand. Icy's hand and nerves were still while his mind raced as he lit the joint.

"I have a business proposition for you Icy Bezel," Santini said as he moved two feet closer to Icy.

Icy coughed but all the while he was thinking of how to reach his other pistol under the bed.

"If you tryna do business with me, tell ya dogs to take these damn red beams off my chest."

The beams disappeared after Santini gave a nod to Mack and Truck. The two men then stepped out from the shadows into Icy's view. Icy saw their mouths watering as Truck and Mack gawked at the two buck naked beauty's sound asleep in Icy's bed.

"I understand that you're in the heroin trade Mr. Bezel," Santini said as he sat on the bed before he continued to speak, "this is your lucky day Mr. Bezel!"

Icy didn't respond. He just listened to the stranger while his mind raced for a way out.

"I can give you access to an unlimited cocaine supply for the 'low-low'." That last statement from the stranger peaked Icy's interest.

"What's the low-low?" Icy asked.

Santini grinned, knowing he had his fish on the hook. "If you agree to my proposal," Santini said looking up to the translucent ceiling, "I can give you kilos for say 25 grand a piece."

Icy knew this deal was too good to be true, keys of cocaine were going for no less than forty to fifty thousand.

"Ok," Icy Bezel said, "what's the catch, what's your proposal...What do I have to do to get that sweet deal?"

Santini stood from the bed then closed the distance between him and Icy Bezel until they were face to face.

"Are you still familiar with your old gang, the Diamond State Mafia?"

CHAPTER 27

King & Queen

Lana beamed with a glow of happiness that came from within. She watched the elderly women of the village apply the traditional bridal tattoos on her body. The ingredients of the red substance were a mystery to all, except a selective few. It was only known and then passed down to a chosen few of Kikuyu women. The elders hummed softly in unison as they applied the ancient scribe and hieroglyphic like images to Lana's skin. Starting at Lana's fingertips, then her hands and on up to the arms until her whole body was covered literally from her head to her toes. Lana closed her eyes and started to hum that same soothing and comforting tune that came from the three gray haired women. Lana thought of her mother and her life during this powerful and spiritual moment. How her mother would be so happy of her only daughter getting married.

"Your finally about to give me a grandbaby!" Lana could hear her mother shouting while laughing.

"I know you would love Kush," Lana said talking to her mother.

Lana didn't have to look far to know that she was blessed to be alive. She had been through countless traumatic and hostile situations. Lana looked down at the severed finger she had suffered by the hands of Niece. She closed her eyes to the oncoming tears when images of dead faces blood and smoke flashed in her mind. She even felt a greedy grumble deep inside her that yearned to wallow in the blood, death and pain. Lana took full responsibility for her mother's death. To her she was just as guilty as the man that pulled the trigger. She just couldn't forgive herself.

Lana pushed the thoughts of all the pain and anguish she had administered as well as suffered out of her head. She inhaled and exhaled slowly visualizing the swoosh and sway of the ocean. She emptied her mind of all the negative thoughts. She repeated to herself all she was grateful of. Her life was dreamy and peaceful now. She lived everyday like a queen. Anything she desired was one snap of the fingers away. Her and Kush had traveled to thirty-two of the fifty-four countries in Africa. Lana had met with kings, queens, chieftains and many other delegators of the people. They had stayed in magnificent gold trimmed palaces to humble thatch roof huts. Lana was mostly grateful for Kush and her health. She laughed to herself with the thought of her health and Kush. Lana hadn't had a mental breakdown in a year in a half. During that time, she almost killed Kush. When Lana snapped back into reality, she had a straight razor pressed against Kush's throat.

"Lana it's me, Kush..." Were the first words she comprehended.

The pressure she held the razor to his neck lightened when she became aware. Kush grabbed Lana's wrist with his left hand then delivered a solid smack to her face.

"Shit Lana! You almost fuckin killed me!" Lana just rubbed the side of her face with a bewildered look.

"I'm sor...," she said reaching for Kush.

"Fuck that sorry shit!" Kush said jumping out of bed. He stayed standing until his blood pressure went down and his heart rate slowed.

"Lana, I'm all you got and you're all I have. I love you...but I can't fuck with you if I gotta worry bout you offing me in my freakin' sleep!"

Lana didn't want to lose Kush. He was right, he was all she had. She didn't fit in MZ Rae's or X's world. Lana loved everything about Kush.

Kush definitely treated and made Lana feel like a queen. She loved the way he looked at her, spoke and listened to her.

"I'll take the medication, Kush." Lana blurted out in tears pleading. Kush knew that Lana didn't like the side effects of the mental health meds and neither did he. Whenever she took the medication it was visibly noticeable with just one look at Lana. It hurt Kush to see Lana in the zombie like state. Lana's beautiful smile, carefree attitude and corky sense of humor all disappeared when she popped the pills. That was the first and last incident where Lana would allow her disorders and conditions to rear its ugly head. After the razor to his neck Kush immediately consulted a holistic doctor for a natural healthier remedy. Kush was referred to Dr. Comar.

The one-armed man wasn't the traditional doctor that you find in the western hemisphere. Comar was a Yoruba spiritualist and herbalist. He lived in the jungles of Masai Mara. Lana had to stay with Dr. Comar in the jungle for three weeks alone. Dr. Comar described to her and Kush that the first week he would clean her spirit and body from all toxins. The second week Comar would focus on a strict herbal diet. Not only introducing natural foods for eating to heal but paste for physical pain and different herbs to burn to calm. For the third week Lana would apply and live by what she'd learned and continue to adhere to the strict diet of earthly foods. A year and a half later to the day Lana still following Dr. Comar's instructions felt like she did before all trauma and pain. Her multiple diagnosis of depression, bipolar disorder and PTSD behaviors were nonexistent. Lana believed with all her heart that she was cured from all the sick thoughts, evil voices and demonic actions.

Tears of joy and thankfulness fell from Lana's face as she thought of how great her life was. Asi interrupted Lana's blissful thoughts.

"You want to hit dis?" Asi asked. Lana opened her eyes to see Asi passing her a blunt. "Are you crying?" Asi asked in broken English.

"No!" Lana said lying. She fanned her face. "It's that sage smoke…it's burning my eyes." Lana smiled when she looked up at Asi.

It always looked funny to see Asi fully garbed smoking weed. The elder women were now scribing on Lana's back. Lana reached for the blunt but Asi hit it again.

"What's the matter?" Lana just continued to smile at her one friend in Africa besides Kush.

Lana met Asi on the second day that Kush and she had arrived in Nairobi. Riding down a busy street in the city Lana saw a woman getting kicked viciously by a man. Lana ordered the driver to stop. The driver complied but looked in the rearview at Kush. Kush hunched his shoulders unaware also of why he was told to stop. Lana jumped out of the Range Rover before it had fully stopped. She didn't even acknowledge the man as he yelled aggressively, standing over the cowering screaming young lady. She just kneeled down and embraced the distraught lady.

"POW!" A single gunshot made Lana and the girl she held jump.

The man that was kicking the girl had raised his hand to strike Lana when she intervened. Before the man's blow could descend, Kush had drawn a .38 revolver and shot him dead, in the heart. Lana took in Asi, a seventeen-year-old orphan. Asi's parents had been murdered three years ago by the terrorist group Al Shabaab. A top member of the group named Joko raped the then fourteen-year-old Asi then made her his girlfriend for about year. After that he sold Asi's body everyday all day.

"So young. So soft and so sweet. Ripe for the pickings!" Joko would say in Swahili to the johns. Ever since that day her and Lana were inseparable.

"I'm just feeling good...just jisikie vizuri!" Lana said in Swahili.

Asi passed the weed to Lana satisfied with the answer. Lana closed her eyes as she hit the marijuana.

"How was school today?" Lana asked Asi.

"It was okay," Asi responded then asked her own question "who's' coming from America for your wedding?"

"Well," Lana said batting her eyes, "my girl MZ Rae is not gonna be able to come, she pregnant. She doesn't want to fly or come to a different country. I understand that," Lana explained receiving the blunt back from Asi.

Lana continued talking after hitting it one time.

"So my aunt Sista Vic that I told you about isn't coming because she taking care of MZ Rae."

Asi just shook her head and asked, "Well, who's coming?" Lana looked at Asi and burst out laughing.

"What?" Asi asked, "Bitch, you are not smarter than me. I know what you want." Lana continued to laugh than began coughing from the weed.

Asi looked puzzled. One of the elders preparing Lana's body tapped her on the shoulder. She was gesturing for Lana to pass her the blunt.

"Aw, here you go moms," Lana said passing it to the old lady, "I didn't know you liked to smoke."

Lana turned to Asi, "Now back to you. My cousin's coming...and he's fine too!" Lana laughed loud looking at Asi. "He's married though!" She laughed even louder then as she continued.

"But one of my homeboys is coming and he if I know, he is single." Asi's face lit up.

"I always dreamed of a handsome American prince making me his wife."

Lana sucked her teeth. "Icy's not a prince but he will show you a good time."

CHAPTER 28

Founding Fathers

X looked out of the window as the Boeing 757 began to descend through the thick clouds. Africa, for the first time during the flight came into view and could be seen below. X starred in awe at the breathtaking view. The colors, even from the high altitude were brilliant and tantalizing to his eyes.

"The Motha Land!" X said out loud to himself.

He instantly thought of his Mother and Grandmother. The butterflies and jitters that had upset his stomach the whole flight long began to subside. Just two days before the wedding is when X made up his mind that he would be attending. He left Evita and his daughter back in Cuba, reluctantly, but sure that it was the right move. He still was a wanted man by the United States government. By the time the plane had touched down at Jomo Kenyatta International airport, a familiar calm had come over X. A sense of relief that only loved ones or the place in one's heart that's considered home, can give a person. He hadn't realized how much he missed his cousin Lana. She was his only blood relative. X still felt responsible for all the pain that Lana had suffered since their reacquaintance. Kush and Icy Bezel were X's only surviving original brothers from The Family. The three of them had come a long way and had been through a lot together.

Every family had disagreements but at the end of the day they were all each other had. When they started The Family as kids, their only objective was getting out of poverty. As they became older their wants and needs grew. By their early twenties the motto was "A million or bust!" Countless

Family members lost their lives on the road to the riches. Now they were rich but not whole. Bloodshed, death and doing things that only God knows took a toll. X would give all of his money back at a drop of a dime if he could chill for a day with Doe, O.G., Lil D, or Sizzle. He would give it all up if he could give that innocence back to Lana. X, Kush, and Lana had a bond that couldn't be broken. Together they had sacrificed their bodies, souls and loved ones to achieve millions.

When X unboarded the plane he was greeted by Africa's intense heat and humidity. A Cuban Madrina of Santeria told X to never wear his traditional black clothes again if he wanted to leave behind his wicked past. Today he wore all white from head to toe. White fedora donned his bald head. A linen white button-down shirt with matching linen white shorts. On his feet X wore old school all white K-Swiss. A thirty-inch diamond encrusted Cuban link chain, Presidential Rolex and pinky ring were the only pieces of jewelry X wore. The diamonds that danced in the sunlight off of each piece of jewelry were the only indicators that he was worth any money. X's head turned side to side as he walked through the terminal. He had never seen so many black people together in one place peacefully. Blacks of all shades of color, from the airport workers to the people catching and unboarding flights.

While waiting for his luggage, X received a tap on his shoulder. To his surprise he turned to see Icy Bezel.

"What's up Bro!" X said before the two men shook hands and hugged.

Icy Bezel always dressed to impress had never changed, if anything he was more flamboyant. Nothing but designer clothes ever adorned Icy Bezel. Today was no different, he wore Gucci everything. His button-down Gucci shirt was cream with red and green strips on the shoulders. The soft shirt lay unbuttoned to Icy's mid chest. X counted at least five chains around Icy's neck. Matching cream crush linen shorts and red and green Gucci flops completed Icy Bezels attire.

"Damn, I thought you was Mr. T!" X said admiring Icy's state of Delaware medallion.

"Boy, you looking good!" Icy said. They shook hands again.

"Family Love, my nigga! Ahhhh!" The two old friends laughed.

"Good to see bro," X said to Icy as he picked his luggage off of the moving conveyer.

"It's good to see you too again, homie," Icy replied to X as they walked out of the airport, "yo, I always knew Kush liked Lana!"

"Did you see this coming?" he asked X.

"Hell nawl!" X said.

"X, I couldn't fuck with Lana. The only way I see her is as the perfect assassin. Shiiiit, she you!"

Before they reached the exit of the airport a tall dark-skinned man yelling "Taxi!" got X's attention. X spotted him out from the many other cab or hack drivers by his Nipsy Hustle t-shirt.

"What kind of ride do you have?" X asked the man. "I have Mar-say-dees." The man said stretching his long arms wide.

"Mercedes?" Icy asked.

"Yes!" the lanky man answered, "my name Lateef." The African said extending his hand to both Icy and X.

"What up," both men said in unison. They followed Lateef down the crowded sidewalk to the Mercedes.

"What did you mean when you said Lana was me?" X asked Icy as they settled into Lateef's Transit. Icy frowned his face up like X was asking a stupid question.

"You built a seductive, calculated and deadly killer," Icy said looking at X, "and I forgot to say Sexy as Hell!"

X's smile faded as Icy's words echoed in his ears. "You built! You built! You built!!!"

"Mobasa," Lateef said as he stopped the Mercedes in front of an eight-foot-high wrought iron gate.

A huge palace could be seen in the distance, behind the wall that surrounded the property. A uniformed ogre of a man came out of a small guard shack.

"What's ya business here?" the big man asked Lateef, the driver.

Icy Bezel answered, "We here to see the bride and groom!"

The guard shook his head no. "Who are you?" The guard asked.

Icy Bezel spat, "We family! Look nigga…" X cut Icy off, seeing that his friend was losing patience.

Bro," X said to guard, "we here for Kush and Lana…your employers. We traveled a great distance for the wedding and if you don't let us through, I'm pretty sure my cousin will fire you from this gravy job."

The guard spoke to Lateef, the driver in Swahili. "They're not here," he said.

"There not here," Lateef said to X and Icy.

"Well, where the fuck they at?" Icy asked.

The guard didn't like Icy Bezel. His nostrils flared as he glared at Icy in the back of the van.

"What the fuck you looking at?" Icy asked aggressively.

The guard spoke to Lateef again in Swahili. Lateef translated what the guard told him because the man wouldn't speak directly to Icy or X in English.

"They are at Zaina Falls," Lateef said.

Icy Bezel looked ice grilled the guard.

"Where the fuck that's at?"

Lateef answered, "Kuhanda Ithigi, it's an African tradition," Lateef said as he backed the van away from the guard shack, "they have it out in the jungle, you know like back in the day shit."

More than an hour and a half later, they still had not arrived to Zaina Falls. Lateef had drove through flat plains where they witnessed seven hyenas attacking a lion. Their journey slowed, as the foliage became thicker and the terrain grew rocky. They continued to ride forty-five minutes even after hearing the ceremonial drums. Once the Mercedes climbed up one last steep hill, Icy and X could see torchlights and people dancing in the distance.

"That's what the fuck I'm talkin' bout!" Icy Bezel said.

X asked the driver Lateef, "How much you charging?"

Putting the truck into park Lateef said, "That will be one hundred American dollars." Lateef was relieved when the men didn't protest the cab fare.

X peeled six twenties from a gold bill clip. Lateef looked around at the spectacle. Dancers in bright colors entertained as people watched from sitting positions.

Lateef said, "Is it alright if I stay here for a minute?"

"Sure," X said as he spotted Lana in the front row to his left. Women surrounded her.

"She's beautiful!" X said to Icy.

"Yes she is," Icy responded, "but she still crazy as hell though."

Lana wore a burgundy head wrap with a matching dress. Gold conch shells decorated her dress.

"Look at this nigga!" Icy said when they saw Kush.

Kush looked regal. He wore the same colors as Lana, a burgundy turban with a dashiki-like shirt. Leopards' skin hung over Kush's neck down around his torso. Kush sat facing Lana fifty yards away with all the males. A slightly elevated dirt plateau, where the dancers performed, was between them. X blew a kiss and Icy waved at Lana as they walked past the hundreds of on lookers.

"Damn," Icy said looking at all the ladies that sat with Lana.

The two men didn't stop until they reached Kush on the groom's side. Kush stood up and greeted his brothers with big hugs. X and Icy sat down on each side of Kush on what felt like a fury carpet. The driver Lateef took a seat in a row of men that sat behind Icy, Kush and X. The men talked and laughed loudly while watching stilt dancers. Moving to the melodic drumbeats, the people drank and smoked bangi.

"Nigga, you still wearing Gucci?" Kush asked Icy Bezel. They had to talk loud because of the drums.

"I ain't gonna never stop wearing it! Them people ain't did shit to me!" Icy said referring to the "black face" turmoil that the company displayed.

Kush passed X a bottle of palm wine. X sipped it timidly at first until tasting the sweet flavor.

"It's good!" X said, "but pass the weed though!" Kush said something to one of the African men sitting behind them.

The man opened a bag full of what looked like rolled joints. "Bangi sticks!" the old man said smiling.

"The tall one right there is my cousin X and the other one is Icy Bezel!" Lana said to Asi as the two ladies watched X and Icy join Kush. "I don't know who that other dude is!" Lana said talking about the driver Lateef.

Asi wore a Kente patterned dress with matching headdress. Her eyes never left Icy Bezel as her and Lana passed a fat bangi stick back and forth.

"Icy Bezel?" Asi asked.

"You introduce us!" Lana laughed.

"He will be my American husband!" Asi dramatically explained to Lana with a flare of her hand. They both laughed.

"Ohoo!" Lana along with everyone watching the acrobatic dancers, groaned at the amazing aerial feat done by two women.

"I'll introduce y'all. You can show him around the city tonight," Lana said exhaling smoke up into the midnight blue havens.

Asi thought out loud, *"I'm gonna give him the tour of the city alright, these sweet African juices!"*

She had never seen a rich single Black American man before. Asi was curious of what a young black American was like. She had been fed the American rhetoric, propaganda and stereotypes all her life. "Boyz N the Hood," "Juice," and "Do the Right Thing," were some of Asi's favorite movies. Her perception of the American Black man was based on the movies she'd watched and the music she'd listened to.

Her and Lana rocked to the heartbeat of the barrel shaped Congo drum and the Ashiko drum. Which was shaped like a cut off cone. Two shirtless men banged on the drums with their hands.

"Man, you shoulda bought Evita," Kush said to X, "let her and Lana start over. Never know. They might need each other one day!"

X looked at the bejeweled bottle of palm wine after taking a swing from it. "I wanted to bring her and the baby but..."

X tilted his head towards Icy Bezel who watched the curvy African women shake their behinds in unison with the drumbeat.

"But, by coming together here we might of sabotaged ourselves!" Kush knew X was talking about Icy Bezel's choice to continue to be in the heroin trade.

"Damn," Kush said shaking his head, "why are you still grinding, Nigga?" Kush asked Icy Bezel.

"What?" Icy said lighting a big joint from the old man's bag. "What the fuck y'all niggas worried about me making money for?" Icy stated with a smirk on his face.

"Because of you," X said, "the muthafuckin' boys could be watching us right now! Why don't you start a business like me and Kush and fly low, under the radar."

Icy replied, blowing smoke out nonchalantly, "I do got my own business like you and X. My shit probably making more money than both all y'all shits put together!" Icy Bezel said laughing as coughed from the weed smoke.

"What boys you talking bout X? The Feds?" Icy asked, "Feds ain't leaving the states." He continued, "the CIA?" X and Kush listened.

"Shiiit, we wasn't that big. We ain't doing no Escobar or Sosa numbers! Them alphabet boys are least of our worries!"

"What the fuck is that supposed to mean?" X snapped.

"Nothing!" Icy Bezel said standing up, "y'all just meet me at your hut eight o'clock sharp!"

X attempted to reach across Kush and grab Icy Bezel. "NO!" Kush said to X, "not here!"

Kush looking at Icy Bezel, "If you've put us in any harm..." Icy brushed Kush off with a wave of his hand.

"I've got this! I'll tell y'all in the morning!"

Asi and Lana felt good from the weed and palm wine. Asi stood up and danced in a circle to hypnotic drumbeats. She kicked the downed feathered pillows.

"Don't hurt nobody girl!" Lana hollered to Asi.

Asi's feet didn't stop moving as she danced up and out onto the natural dirt stage. She gyrated her hips and beat the ground with bare feet until she ended up directly in front of the standing Icy Bezel. When Icy Bezel looked up, his eyes locked with Asi's. She began to slowly wind her hips seductively, her eyes never leaving his. Asi danced with a fire and aggression. Sensuality poured from Asi's choreography. Some of the African men laughed while others stood up to pat Icy Bezel on the back.

"They're saying congratulations!" Lateef yelled to Icy Bezel.

"Congratulations for what?" Icy Bezel asked.

Lateef laughed. "You've just been claimed! That was a courting or mating dance!"

X and Kush joined in the laughter. X allowed himself to relax on his exterior. But inside he had a feeling he shouldn't have come. At this exact moment X regretted ever leaving his real family.

"I've gotta get the fuck home!"

CHAPTER 29

Fail Switch

When George Rodgers, otherwise known as Santini, arrived in Kenya, his first stop was the American Embassy. His men Truck and Mack had arrived two days before to run surveillance and monitor the Diamond State Mafia's every move. Icy Bezel had previously disclosed to Santini the location of where and when the wedding would take place. He didn't trust Icy Bezel no further than he could throw him. Santini had already blessed Icy Bezel and upheld his end of the deal. For the last three months Icy Bezel has been reaping the rewards of having the best product at the lowest cost, courtesy of Santini. Even with reports back from Mack and Truck confirming everything that Icy Bezel said was the truth, Santini still couldn't one hundred percent trust the man. For that fact, he compiled all of the evidence he had gained as a Federal Agent on each member of the Diamond State Mafia and delivered the dossier to the front gate of the U.S. Embassy. Santini also informed the Embassy that the very same criminal organization was in their own beautiful city of Nairobi.

Foreign Service Officer Harlee Terrell was eating lunch at his desk at 12:15 p.m. Eastern Africa Time.

"Hey!" Andrew Wright said as he knocked two times while walking in to Harlee's office, "aren't you from Delaware?"

Harlee didn't answer right away as he chewed his lunch. He had been ridiculed often by his co-workers about the size of his birthplace.

"Why?" Harlee asked.

Andrew threw a small stack of papers on Harlee's desk. "Thought this would be good for you," Andrew said as watched Harlee skim over a few pages of the documents he bought in.

"Where did you get this from?" Harlee asked.

"Somebody just dropped it off on our doorstep," Andrew said before asking, "are you familiar with these people?"

Of course, Harlee was familiar with the infamous Diamond State Mafia, everyone from Delaware or the surrounding states were.

"Yes, I know the case," Harlee replied still reading over the pages. "They're here?!" Harlee stated.

Andrew wasn't sure if Harlee was asking him or telling him that the Diamond State Mafia were on Kenyan soil.

"Yes. They're here," Andrew informed him, "and it's your case now. Good luck." Andrew turned to leave the office.

"Hold up. I'm an Economic Officer, what am I supposed to do with this?" Andrew spun around with a sigh.

"These guy's and gal's net worth are well into the millions. Five to six million to be almost exact," Andrew said now stepping back into the office and closing the door behind him, "I figured this case would be great for your future career in politics. You do plan on going back to your state to serve as a representative of the people?"

Harlee replied, "Yes."

Andrew smiled showing coffee stained teeth. "Well, what better way is there to show your beloved Delawareans that you're the best man for mayor, governor, or even a senator's seat!" Andrew paused, knowing Harlee had dreams of being a public server.

"Harlee Terrell!" Andrew said cupping his hands over his mouth for an echo effect, "one of your very own, Delaware.

The man who traveled abroad to bring back the ruthless organization that committed murder and profited millions from drugs in our dear state of Delaware!"

Harlee closed his eyes and could see himself taking the podium to speak after being elected senator. Andrew clearing his throat interrupted his daydream.

"Uuh Uugh Hmm! Get with the Inspector General of the Kenya National Police and go get these assholes before they disappear!"

CHAPTER 30

American Thug

Asi wasn't disappointed in her expectations of Icy Bezel. After the wedding ceremony, Lana introduced her to Icy Bezel. Icy actually exceeded Asi's assumptions of an American thug. Asi volunteered to show Icy Kenya's nightlife. Lana and Kush by wedding traditions weren't permitted to see one another again until the wedding. Kush retired to the groom's hut drunk off from palm wine. Lana had her own hut as well, both built by the locals for the occasion. X went back to Lana's hut. The two talked, laughed and even cried together late into the night.

Icy Bezel and Asi danced until their feet hurt in the world-renowned Black Diamond nightclub. She and Icy took pictures in front of the lion inside the club chained. Asi was turned on by the confidence and bravado of Icy Bezel. His hip-hop and street swagger was the epitome of what she imagined an American thug to be. She was captivated by Icy. Asi definitely had Icy's attention as well. He couldn't keep his hands off of her silky jet-black skin. Before long they were heading back to Icy's hotel.

They had some amazing and prolonged foreplay. Icy made Asi put on her Niqab, the traditional Muslim women garment that covered the body and face showing nothing but her eyes. He told her they could role-play. He would be the American solider and she a possible suicide bomber. It wasn't long before he had Asi stripped naked wearing only her veil, concealing her face. The two had incredible sex. Asi collapsed on Icy Bezel's chest drenched in sweat and sticky from bodily fluids. She woke up an hour later to an empty bed and muffled voices coming from the balcony. Icy thought nothing of it when he returned to his bed to see Asi was gone.

It was almost five in the morning when Asi reached Lana's hut. Lana's anxiety wouldn't allow her to sleep. She couldn't believe that she would be a married woman in less than ten hours. Lana was nervous but also elated. She couldn't remember the last time she felt this good. Asi's knocks were barely heard over Lana singing to a Beyoncé song playing from her iPhone. She wiped tears from her eyes before pulling back the heavy Kenya blanket that was acting as a door. Between crying and laughing she had been smoking fat bangi sticks all night into the morning. Lana went back to admiring her naked body in a big mirror made of camel bone and thuya wood.

"You have a good time?" Lana asked, "I've been waiting for you girl."

It registered to Lana that something was wrong a split second before she looked up, because normally her friend's mouth would be running.

"Sister, I have something to tell you," Asi said grabbing a silk robe and covering Lana's shoulders.

"What's wrong?" Lana asked, her tone going flat.

"Icy Bezel…"

Lana blurted out, "He hit you?"

Asi shook her head. "NO!...But I heard him talking to a colonizer!"

Lana closed the small distance to Asi. Inches from her face Asi felt like Lana was peering through her soul. "Did you hear what was said?" Lana asked.

Asi shook her head tears welling up in her eyes. "Yes." Asi said stifling her cry. "They are planning on killing you, Kush and your cousin tomorrow…"

Lana answered with a grunt, "HUUHH!" Lana walked over to a small table that held her solitary cards and a couple of already rolled joints. "Kill 'em," she said quietly as she lit a banga stick.

Asi looked like a gazelle feeling the first flesh-piercing bite of a lioness.

"WHA-WHAT did you say?" Asi asked, knowing her ears didn't deceive her.

Twenty minutes later in the in a Nairobi hotel, a knock at Icy Bezel's door interrupted his morning workout. He looked through the peephole and smiled. The time it took him to unlock the door and open it, he had a boner.

"I was just thinking about that good juice box!" Icy said as he watched the garbed woman enter the room.

She raked her fingers across his bare chest and down to the semi-erect briefs.

"I knew you was coming back," Icy said as he allowed her to pull him over to the bed. "Aw you ready too!" Icy said with a smile as she pushed him back on the bed.

Icy bit down on his lip and his face hardened at the first sensational feeling of his rod being engulfed slowly. He laid back and put his hands behind his head.

"Damn, you was holding back on me earlier," Icy's voice trembled, "I just might take you with me!" He shook as he climaxed, "MMMMM!" Icy moaned and stretched.

His penis stayed semi-heavy as the agile lady climbed on top of him. She giggled as her hot vagina welcomed Icy's hardness.

"Take this off," Icy said snatching off the veil.

His body froze during mid stroke as he looked into the Queen B's face. Lana laughed.

"I have a confession," Lana said as she slowly moved up and down on Icy's pole. On every down stroke Lana would grind in a circular motion. "I Just had to fuck you before I got married…"

Icy Bezel's body relaxed and he allowed a mischievous grin to spread across his face.

"I KNEW you always wanted this!" Icy said confidently.

Lana opened up what looked like a small hand-held makeup kit while she just sat with Icy's penis throbbing in her trimmed vagina. She held the pink compact in front of her mouth.

"I doubt it!" she said in response to Icy's last comment.

"Wheeew!" Lana blew hard into the case.

Black dust flew into Icy's eyes and mouth. Lana jumped up fast as he began kicking and swinging.

"Bitch!" Icy streamed, "I'm gonna kill yo' scandalous ass!" Icy stumbled blindly around the room, swinging haymakers in the air trying to strike Lana.

"YOU the bitch, snake!" Lana said, "Fuck me! I wanna know how you gonna turn your back on Kush and X?"

Trying to lunge in the direction he heard Lana's voice coming from, Icy fell to the carpet.

"Don't bother tryna move again, cause it won't happen," Lana talked as she walked over to the defenseless Icy Bezel, "that little concoction that I blew in your eyes and mouth is something I created."

Icy's body began to seize up. He looked frightened. His eyes darted all around in a panicked manner. He tried to speak. "I-I-I WASSS GON TE-TELL Y'ALL..." The deadly venom had paralyzed everything except Icy's eyes.

"I'm proud of myself," Lana said stopping to smile in the middle of searching the room for Icy's phone. "I crystalized the venoms of the Black Mamba and Green Mamba. Then I grinded them up then mixed it with cornmeal and chili powder." Lana found an iPhone and two old untraceable flip phones.

"Now who the fuck have you been talking to?" Lana said stealing one last look at the suffocating Icy Bezel.

CHAPTER 31

Can't Stay Away

Kush tossed and turned on the small cot in his hut.

"Fuck!"

He missed his bed and he yearned for Lana's touch. He was all for getting back to his roots but this was too far. He hadn't had any of Lana's goodies in a week.

"I'm tired of jerking off and my lady is right next door!" Kush spoke out loud as he put on his pants and shoes, "Fuck Dr. Comar right now!"

Five minutes later as roosters crowed at the brightening of the horizon, Kush slipped into Lana's hut.

"SPZZZ!" Kush said to the sleeping figure covered by a single blanket.

Kush rubbed on Asi's hips and butt, "You getting thick, Bae."

Kush whispered as he placed a kiss at the nape of her neck. He kissed her again as he moved up to Asi's ear. All the while his eyes were closed and his hand between Asi's legs. Asi's eyes popped opened when she felt her pussy getting stroked.

"Hey, Lanie," Kush called softly again, "give me a kiss, I miss you."

Asi jumped up. "No! No. Noo!" she yelled.

Kush pulled the heavy covering away from the door so the light of the day would allow him to see in the small hut. Kush saw that it was Asi.

"Where the fuck is Lana?!"

Kush made Asi tell him every detail she could remember about Icy Bezel 's conversation with the mystery White man.

"How long has Lana been gone?" Kush asked while ransacking the hut.

"About a half an hour," Asi answered. Kush continued to search around through Lana's things in the hut.

"Asi!" he called out, "go to my hut and get my brotha X!"

Ten minutes later Asi and X walked into Lana's hut. Kush was now lifting up the single sized cot.

"What's up Kush?" X asked looking worried. He looked around the tossed hut. "Where's Lana?"

Kush stopped in his tracks. "Going to kill Icy!"

X closed the gap between him and Kush fast.

"Icy is trying to set us up." Seeing X was coming at him aggressively, Kush dropped the small cot and stood his ground.

"I just got here, X. I just found out she was gone!"

X's face looked demonic as he and Kush stared at each other. "What the fuck are you still doing here?" X asked Kush.

He turned to Asi. "Take me to my cousin."

"Hold up!" Kush said as he checked behind a mask of Ogun that hung on the mud and clay walls. "I knew she had some heat somewhere in here." Kush checked the clip of a 9-millimeter.

"Let's GO!"

CHAPTER 32

Second, First Impressions

Directly next door to Icy Bezel's room, in the same hotel were Santini, Mack, and Truck. The three men sat fully dressed around a rectangular coffee table that was peppered with guns and ammo. The room smelled of Marlboro smoke and days old rotting food. Metallic clicks and clinking could be heard every now and again over a Lynyrd Skynyrd song that played at a low volume. Santini blew in the cylinder of his forty-five-caliber revolver as he cleaned the black gun. Mack and Truck were busy cleaning and inspecting their sniper rifles when Santini's phone received a text message. "JUST GOT SM INFO U SHUD KNO"

"Mack," Santini said throwing his phone back on the table after reading the text, "go out on the balcony and see what our man Icy Bezel wants."

Truck and Santini shared a laughed of his pronunciation of Icy's name. Mack smacked his lips and shook his head as he dropped the rifle down hard on the table. He scoffed as he walked to the glass sliding door.

"Next time, just tell him to walk out of his room and come over!" Mack slid open the door and stuck his head out of it.

"AAAAAHHH!" he screamed seconds later.

Mack snatched down the vertical blinds in an attempt to back away from the door. Blood squirted from Mack's neck onto the blinds, walls and carpet. He stomped around in pain, panic and shock. Falling to his knees the big man's hands clawed at the clean and precise wound the blood poured from.

Truck screamed as he watched his brother's body thud to the floor.

With blind rage at seeing his brother die right before his eyes, Truck let off a barrage of shots from the semi-automatic rifle he was cleaning.

"UGHHH!" Truck let out a sorrowful war cry as he squeezed the trigger.

The 223 caliber bullets shredded the blinds and riddled the glass doors of the balcony.

"Stop! Stop fucking shooting!" Santini yelled to the blood thirsty Truck.

Truck didn't stop shooting until his magazine went empty. Aware that they were sitting ducks, Santini shot out the only light in the room. Enabling anyone from seeing into the room from the balcony, Santini could only hear Truck reloading his weapon and crying in the silence that followed the repeated booming shots.

"Hey, soldier!" Santini snapped at Truck, "get ya shit together!" Truck continued to cry for his brother Mack. "You coming in now?" Santini yelled out to the dark balcony.

No one responded. Truck's sniffles were all that could be heard by Santini. But he was sure that someone was still out there.

"This is not the work of those shooting ass Diamond Mafia yahoo's...is it?" Santini said as he army crawled closer to the balcony, taking cover bchind a love seat. He continued to speak, positive that someone was out there listening.

"Is that you Kalana?"

Santini gave a hand command to Truck to approach the balcony. They both slowly and quietly inched closer to the glassless door.

"Silent. Quiet and deadly!" Santini said, "I'm thrilled to have seen firsthand the work of the Queen Bitch!" Confident that he was speaking to Lana, "You might don't remember me." Santini continued, "but we met more than a few times."

Santini gave a command for Truck to go through the tattered blinds out onto the balcony. The shattered glass from the sliding door rained down all over Lana. After slicing Trucks neck Lana didn't have time to jump back over to Icy's balcony. When Mack started cutting loose with the rifle Lana had time only to drop down on the balcony's floor. She covered her eyes with the long cloak of Asi's Niqab. During the silence that followed the barrage of bullets, Lana dared not move a muscle. Her heart skipped a beat when she heard a familiar voice, a voice that haunted her dreams. Lana's mind and focus switched.

The violent reality of the here and now took a back seat to her confused subconscious. Lana's mind searched franticly for answers.

"Am I Imagining this?" "Is that voice real?" Lana tried with all her might and will to put a face to that voice.

When Rodger's weathered face popped into Lana's mind she opened her eyes. Through the thin cloth of the garment she saw a man's boot stepping onto the balcony. Lana lifted her legs up bringing her knees to her chest then kangaroo kicked Truck with both feet.

"Oooff!" Santini watched Truck fly backwards back into the hotel room.

Lana did a rising handspring, jumping from her back to her feet then tumble rolled into the room. A small couch stopped Truck's backward momentum. As soon as he regained his composure Truck fired blindly around the dark room trying to hit the cat-like black figure.

"Stop it!" Santini said tackling Truck to the floor.

The two men strained their eyes peering around the dark room. Sirens could be heard in the distance clearly from the shot-out patio doors.

CHAPTER 33

Kill or Be Killed

Kush was first through Icy Bezel's hotel room door, followed by X and Asi.

"DAMN!" X and Kush said in unison while looking down at the contorted face and naked body of Icy Bezel.

Icy's face was twisted and his tongue stuck out of his mouth like a dead frog.

Asi shrieked at the horrific sight burying her head in X's chest. "You snake muthafucka!" Kush yelled kicking Icy Bezel's stiff corpse.

"Where the fuck is my cousin?" X said not directing the comment to anyone. His question was answered seconds later.

"BOOF--BOF-BOF-BOF-BOF..." Ear splitting gunfire caused X, Kush and Asi to all jump down on the floor for cover.

After the gunfire deceased it was dead silent. Kush, X and Asi didn't move right away from their cover on the floor next to Icy's dead body. A man yelling in the next room broke the silence. They heard the unknown man say Lana's name. Kush cocked the nine-millimeter as X bolted out the room. When Kush reached X outside the door of the next room, more shots were being fired from inside. X kicked down the door thinking only of Lana.

"BOOM!" X stood still trying to see in the dark room.

From inside the room Truck aimed his rifle at X who was an easy target standing still in the lit hallway. X saw the flash from the rifle's muzzle. The shot hit the ceiling.

"Shit!" X said closing his eyes.

He heard someone struggling and scuffling. As his eyes adjusted to the darkness of the room he could make out the big fellow that shot at him being engulfed by a black blob. Kush pushed passed X aiming his pistol at the lone person standing inside the room.

"Hold!" X said to Kush, "Don't shoot!" X could see that there was someone on the back of the man holding the rifle.

"Lana!" X said to himself.

Lana held on for dear life onto Truck's neck and back. She tried desperately to slice Truck's neck with the straight razor she used on his brother. He bucked and thrashed trying to throw Lana off his back but to no avail. Truck backed up against a wall, using all of his weight and a burst of momentum as hard as he could. That caused Lana to drop the straight razor. Lana was no match for the big muscular Truck without her razor. His massive neck was too thick for her to choke him.

Truck manage to raise his rifle and bust two more shots recklessly in X's direction. X dove to the floor for cover as Kush kneeled down to one knee aiming at the big man's legs. Lana struggled to remove the veil from her mouth. Once she had it pulled down to her chin she sunk her teeth in Trucks carotid artery.

"ΛΛHHHH!" Truck screamed.

"BOOM! BOOM! BOOM!" Kush shot Truck's knees and thighs. Santini eased out of the room by way of the balcony during all the chaos. He didn't have to wait around to know that Truck was a dead man.

Kush found a working light. When he cut the light on he saw Lana on the big man's back as he laid on his stomach. She still had a lock onto the dead mans' throat.

"Fuck, Lana!" X said looking at his cousin with sympathy.

"Turn that fucking light off!" a bloody mouth Lana yelled at Kush.

Before Kush could cut them back off, two shots were fired from the balcony. X went down face first. Kush screamed as he emptied out the clip of the nine into the balcony. The police sirens were close. Reflections of red emergency lights danced on the walls of the dark room.

CHAPTER 34

The Sacrifice

"XXXXXXXXXX!" Lana yelled, her face smeared red and warm blood dripped from her mouth. She ran over to X and rolled him over.

"Come on, Bro," Kush said, "were you hit?"

X grunted out, "Hell yeah!"

Kush searched X's body. He discovered two wounds. X had taken shots in the chest and neck.

Asi finally came over from Icy Bezel's room once the shooting stopped. She covered her month when she saw the bloody X being hoisted up by Lana and Kush.

"You gonna be alright, Bro," Kush whispered to his best friend. X forced a smile. "Y'all niggas getting me shot all the way over here in Africa," X said weakly with a smile.

"Asi!" Lana spat, "Go get the car. Pull up to the door!"

As Asi bolted out of the room, Kush and Lana carried X to the elevator. X's dead weight made it difficult for the two of them to lift him. Once the elevator reached the first floor Lana and Kush could see the Kenyan National Police skidding to a stop in front of the hotel. Kush picked X up in a fireman's carry on his shoulder.

"Back door!" Kush and Lana said together.

X grunted in pain with every step Kush took. Lana pushed the emergency door open then peeked out to see if the coast were clear. The alley was deserted. She held it open for Kush and X. No sooner than she let the door close behind them Asi was speeding toward them.

"Right on time," Kush said, "we gonna get you to the hospital Bro, hold on." Black and white police cars sped behind Asi in Kush's white Range Rover.

"Oh shit!" Lana said, "hurry!"

When Asi screeched to a halt alongside Lana, Kush and X, the KNP were five seconds behind. Lana got in the back seat and slid over. Kush threw X in the back seat with her and closed the door.

"Get out of here!" Kush hollered.

Asi not aware that Kush wasn't in the truck, squealed off headed for the hospital.

Kush stood in the middle of the small alley blocking the cops. He pointed the empty nine-millimeter pistol at the oncoming authorities. Tires burned rubber as three squad cars stopped. Two police hopped out and took cover behind their cars.

"You got me!" Kush yelled out throwing his pistol down to the ground.

"I give up!" Kush said smiling.

Kush's smile faded when he heard the policemen laughing. One of the officers yelled in Swahili.

"MOTOOOO!"

CHAPTER 35

Bunduki Waathirika – A Victim in Swahili

The sky was full of colors at morning's first light, as Asi sped down Kenya's sparse roads pushing seventy miles an hour. It took her 12 minutes and 51 seconds to go 15 miles. The Range Rover lunged forward as Asi snatched the SUV in park. They were in front of the Kenyatta National Hospital. Asi ran through the emergency doors screaming help in Swahili.

"MSAADA! MSAADA!" Lana tried with great difficulty to get X out of the back seat.

"Come on, Cuz. We here," Lana coaxed, "you gonna be good."

She bore the brunt of X's weight, as his long arm drooped heavily around her neck. On the forth step she took, Lana dropped down to one knee. In tears Lana grunted loudly as she stood back up. She took three more wobbly steps before her and X crashed to the ground. Thirty seconds later Asi was back with nurses, orderlies and a stretcher. They carefully placed X on the stretcher as Asi helped Lana up.

"Bunduki waathirika!" One nurse yelled as they rushed X into the hospital.

Lana and Asi trailed behind X until he was whisked through double doors that read chumba cha upasuaji. There, a short man in glasses wearing a white doctor's coat told them they couldn't go any further. Lana sat in the waiting room while Asi went to use the bathroom then outside to move the Range Rover.

"I'll be right back. I'll bring you some coffee back." Lana shook her head slightly as she looked up sadly at Asi. Asi grabbed Lana and hugged her tight.

Kenya National Police arrived to the hospital minutes after Lana, X and Asi. When Asi exited the hospital to move the Range Rover two police cars were parked around it. One to the front and the other at its rear, prevented anyone from moving the truck. All four doors were open on the SUV as an officer in a green uniform searched through it.

Asi thought, "*I must have missed them when I went to the restroom.*" She gasped, "Kalana."

"*How could this be happening? Is this REALLY happening to me? This ain't happening!*"

Lana sat in the chair with her hands in her lap staring into space. Her fingers never stopped moving, fidgeting together constantly. The crackling of a radio instantly silenced all the questioning voices in her head. Lana stood up and peaked around the corner. Two police officers were talking to the desk nurse. Lana ducked back into the waiting room just as the nurse began to point in her direction.

"Shit!" Lana said running to the window.

She hadn't gone up any stairs but she was on the second floor. There was another roof a floor below. Lana slid the big window open then kicked the screen out. She immediately climbed out of the window. Lana hung from a ledge under the window. To minimize the length of her long jump She tried to stretch her body out as long as she could before letting her fingers slip off. Lana fell hard and awkward on the stoned roof twisting her ankle.

She hit the ground running in pain. Almost immediately after her feet touched the ground, voices speaking Swahili could be heard at the window. She didn't look back as she ran as fast as she could to the edge of the roof. The Kenyan police had not long before upgraded their outdated weapons. The newly Spanish made, CZ Scorpion EVO A1 airsoft rifles was a sub machine gun. The officers loved to use their new toys. Automatic fire rang out from the window. A stream of bullets being shot in three shot burst trailed behind Lana ricocheting off the stones on the roof. Lana had no time to hesitate. The bullets forced her to run off the edge of the roof. A thick wall of brown Brabant hedges broke her fall. Lana quickly climbed out of the hedges and disappeared in the throbbing workforce fueling Nairobi's booming economy.

CHAPTER 36

Four Months Later

MZ Rae hadn't spoken to Lana since the day before the wedding. After not hearing from Lana on the day of the wedding and the days that followed, MZ Rae began to worry. Her worries that something bad had happened were confirmed while watching CNN a week later. The news anchor said four unidentified American men were found dead in Nairobi, Kenya.

Terrance had been in Nairobi searching for Lana. If he didn't insist on going to Africa to find Lana, MZ Rae would of went herself baby and all. When Terrance arrived to Nairobi, he first went to Kush and Lana's house. The guard shack was empty and the gate was open. Terrance walked cautiously up the house valet style driveway. The property was vandalized and unkempt. Windows were busted out. The house had been stripped of anything valuable or worth something. Music played from a room upstairs. Terrance walked quietly through the house. The house smelled of urine and feces. He slowed up the closer he approached the music. He stopped at a closed door assuming it was the bathroom. He turned the knob but it was locked. Before he could raise his hand to knock, he felt a cold piece of steel pressed up against his face.

Terrance was spun around slowly before he was facing a shirtless African man. He only wore some cutoff jeans and flip-flops.

"Gimme your money!" The tall dread's hands were stretched up high to the ceiling.

"Alright, Brothaman! I'm getting my wallet."

Terrance slowly reached in his pants pocket and came out with a

Giorgio Armani buckskin wallet. He slowly extended his hands out to the man with a killer's scowl. The man snatched the wallet from Terrance and stuffed it in his own pockets.

"You don't want my shoes?" Terrance asked.

The man looked down to Terrance's Michael Jordan's number 12 sneakers. At that moment Terrance came up with a right upper cut to the man's chin.

"CRACK!" The man was knocked unconscious by the quick phantom punch.

Terrance picked up the man's discarded pistol and fished through the snoring man's pocket to retrieve his wallet back.

Two months later Terrance was still in Nairobi. He had been up and down the streets and every establishment showing Lana's picture. He wanted to go home. He missed his baby, MZ Rae and the serenity of Venice. The night before he had smoked his last spliff of weed that he had brought with him.

"Ganji?" Terrance asked mimicking smoking by putting two fingers up to his mouth.

The young African's attire was East Coast Hip Hop, baggy jeans and Timberlands. Terrence stopped to the young man because he had caught a whiff of ganji when he walked past him. The boy sat on a parked mopad talking on a phone. The kid unzipped a fanny pack around his waist. Buds of weed spelled out as he shoved his hand into it. The boy came out with a fist full of ganji.

"Twenty shillings." Terrance gave him fifty shillings.

Terrance pulled out his rolling papers right there on the spot. It wasn't until he finished rolling his beloved "ganji" and attempted to light the fat spliff that he looked up. He did a double take at a lady that looked just like Lana, across the street sitting on a barstool.

"Look, I know what I am talking about Baby!" Terrance reassured MZ Rae, "that's her! It's her in the picture I sent to you right?"

"Alright, alright, Imma say something!"

Terrance walked up to the lady that sat on a stool in front of a pool hall. She was smoking a joint but what Terrence smelled wasn't just marijuana. He kept MZ Rae on the cell phone while he approached the woman.

"Excuse me, Kalana Watson?"

The lady in the cheap satin dress looked up at the tall dreadlocked Terrence. A small hint of a smile began to form but vanished. She said nothing. Terrance looked into her bloodshot reddened eyes. Terrance was positive that this lady was Lana, even though she looked slightly different. To him her face looked harder and much older than the picture of her that was on his phone just taken five months ago.

"You want her?" a tall dark skinned, lanky man with piercings on his face and sporting a red Mohawk asked.

"Sixty dollar, half an hour," the man only known as Dirtbike explained.

"A ben-ji-men for de hour."

Terrance looked back to Lana pitifully. Sadden by the proposal and the reality of what Lana had been put through.

"Lana!" Terrance yelled.

Hoping to snap her back to herself. He had only met Lana once, briefly but knew something was wrong.

"Ah Captain?" Dirtbike said, "her name is Action! Because she don't talk, she all action! Ha! Ha! Ha! Ha!" Dirk said laughing, "One American hundred and you can take her upstairs!"

Terrance wanted to beat Dirtbike to a pulp, but he knew that would be suicide for him. A husky fellow in a vest with no shirt on, sat at the entrance of the bar with a sawed-off double barrel.

"O.K.," Terrance said to the Mohawk man.

Dirtbike grinned showing he had a gold crown. Dirtbike shook his head to the man at the door, which then stood up and moved to the side, clearing the entrance for Terrance. Terrance dug into his pockets and took out two 100$ bills.

"2 hours," Terrance said.

Terrance gave the money to Dirtbike, then grabbed Lana's hand leading her into the bar.

The bar resembled the saloons in the old west. It had a long mahogany bar and about 5 round tables in the dim lit brothel. Rooms were upstairs for paying customers. Terrance held Lana's hand until they walked in the barely furnished room. A bed, vanity mirror and one chair were all that was in the room. Terrance pulled out his phone and called MZ Rae back. He handed the phone to Lana, who took it slowly. Lana pressed the phone to her ear and listened. Within the first minute of her listening, tears started to roll down Lana cheeks...

"I'll call you back when I have her on de plane," Terrence said to MZ Rae ending the call immediately.

He grabbed both of Lana's hands and looked into her eyes. Her bloodshot eyes were half opened and glassed over. Lana looked past the big six-four three-hundred-pound frame of Terrance like he wasn't even in the room.

"Crosses!" Terrance swore.

He held Lana's hands firmly and pulled her to him. Getting her attention. Lana tensed up as his grip tightened up on her hands. She looked up at the big man with dreads. Their eyes met.

"You hear, Lana? I'm getting you outta here, taking you to MZ Rae!" Terrence said in a low tone but aggressive.

He released his hold when her eyes showed awareness. She looked at Terrence angrily. The Rasta just looked down at Lana quietly waiting for a reaction. He anticipated resistance and noncompliance but Lana replied simply, "O.K."

"No! No! No!" Dirtbike said as Terrance attempted to walk out of the bar together holding hands. The burly man at the door stuck his leg across the exit door and put his hand on the pistol grip of the sawed-off shotgun standing in the corner beside him.

"Where yo gon?" Dirtbike spat as he stood up removing a white pair of sunglasses.

His red Mohawk made him look and seem even taller. Terrence still held Lana's hand tight. He backed up so he could see Dirtbike and the Doorman at the same time.

"Dis mi Sista!" Terrence said to Dirtbike, looking back and forth.

"Sister?" Dirtbike questioned looking puzzled.

"Dada!" The man at the door said.

Terrance turned back to the man hearing him speak for the first time. Now the man had the shotgun in his hand. Dirtbike and the man spoke back and forth in Swahili. Both men sounded agitated to Terrance as his head snapped back and forth between the two. Lana eyes had glazed over and barely looked opened, Terrence felt her body sway and teeter. Dirtbike banged his fist down on the bar hard. Terrance didn't speak Swahili but he read body language. He reasoned that Lana leaving could be their only disagreement. Terrance held his hands up.

"Dirtbike!" He went for his pockets slowly.

The sentry pumped and aimed the gage at Terrance. Terrance had still hands as he dug into the two lower pockets of camouflage army fatigues. He pulled out two rolls of U.S. currency. He tossed one to Dirtbike and then one to the doorman with the shotgun. Terrance grabbed Lana's hand and shot through the door as Dirtbike and the shotgun man counted their loot.

CHAPTER 37

Alive on Arrival - Lana

Three hours later Lana lay sound asleep on a leer jet owned by MZ Rae, headed for Venice, Italy. Terrance was on the phone with MZ Rae explaining to her that Lana was fine. He left out the part that Lana was a "street walker" and how he paid five thousand dollars to a guy with a Mohawk named Dirtbike and a man with a shotgun to get Lana.

"Thank you Jesus!" MZ Rae cried out.

Terrance continued, "I gave her some Estazolam, she should sleep the whole flight. One more thing," Terrence said, "I think she's been smoking Whoonga. It's a mixture of ganji, heroin, Stocrin and rat poison!"

Tears flowed down MZ Rae's face. "Just bring her home, we'll take care of her…" X.

At the exact same time, on the other side of the world, an airplane with eight inmates aboard circled Dover, Delaware's Airforce Base. Through the eye slits of a plastic mask X watched the iconic forty-six-foot monster outside the speedway. X was being transported in restraints similar to the ones Hannibal Lecter wore. He was classified as High Risk. X never thought he would ever step foot back in Delaware or the United States for that matter. Even under the circumstances, he was happy to be back. After spending a month in a Nairobi hospital he was transferred to Kamiti Downs. When X woke up in the hospital he was already chained to the bed. Both of his feet were shackled to the bed rails on both sides.

"Damn, I'm still living?" X asked, gently lifting up the gaze on his chest.

He looked at the bullet hole that had already started to scab over. X hanked his deceased Mother, Grandmother, and all his ancestors. He knew that someone or someone's were watching over him. He looked around and saw he was in an open ward. There were about 25 to 30 people in the huge room. A Kenyan policemen reading a newspaper sat at the foot of X's bed. X's whole body hurt. He had a bandage on his neck and one in the center of his chest. X thought and plotted his escape but was to weak. When he finally began to feel strong enough for his escape he was shipped out to Kamiti Downs.

Kamiti Downs was the worst place X had ever been. Everything was terrible, the food, water, cleanliness and living conditions. The guards were brutal with entitlements and the inmates were savages full of rage. Still recuperating from a neck and chest gunshot wound X feared for his life. He faked that his injuries were more severe and hurt more than they did. He would secretly build his core everyday while at Kamiti. Anticipating the day when one of the Africans would try him. He walked slow and with a wooden cane. Hoping lameness and being handicapped would discourage inmates from antagonizing. The maximum-security prison was overcrowded and filthy. The living conditions were poor and the treatment inhumane. X was positive that he would die in Kamiti Downs, if not from disease then by murder. Lucky for X that Kamiti Down's computer systems are the jails most reliable asset. It took twenty-nine days for the Kamiti officers to get X's prints. As soon as X's prints were placed in the Integrated Automated Fingerprint Identification System a Red Notice by INTERPOL was placed on Yusef Watson. The very next day the international warrant for X was carried out. Two INTERPOL officers picked X up and the extradition, to his delight, begun.

"Once again it's on!" X said to himself when the plane landed.

He took in a deep breath. He tried not to think about Evita or his baby girl Ximena. X was just grateful for the time they had shared together and the fact that he could set them up so they never would have to worry about money. His great-great grand kids will still be eating from him. That thought still put a smile on his face in the midst of the despair.